Do They Exist?

Do Dragons Exist?

Gail Snyder

ReferencePoint Press®

San Diego, CA

ReferencePoint Press®

For more information, contact:
ReferencePoint Press, Inc.
PO Box 27779
San Diego, CA 92198
www.ReferencePointPress.com

LIBRARY OF CONGRESS CATALOGING-IN-PUBLICATION DATA

Snyder, Gail.
Do dragons exist? / by gail snyder.
pages cm. -- (Do They Exist?)
Includes bibliographical references and index.
Audience: Grade: 9 to 12.
ISBN-13: 978-1-60152-854-4 (hardback)
ISBN-10: 1-60152-854-X (hardback)
1. Dragons--Juvenile literature. I. Title.
GR830.D7S67 2016
398.24'54--dc23

2015018997

Contents

Introduction

Dragons: Myths or Misunderstandings?

In 2009 right before they were due to play one of their early gigs, members of a Las Vegas–based independent rock 'n' roll band were searching for a new name for their group. The four members of the group, vocalist Dan Reynolds, bassist Ben McKee, guitarist Wayne Sermon, and drummer David Platzman, settled on Imagine Dragons, a name based on shuffling the letters in a number of the band's favorite words. Reynolds recalls, "To be honest with you, when we were scrambling up the letters to come up with Imagine Dragons, I don't even remember how we actually decided that was the name. It just kind of stuck. We were just like, 'Yeah, that sounds like a cool name.' We had a gig like two days later, and there we were."[1]

That the members of the Grammy award–winning band find themselves at a loss to explain why they latched on to the symbolism of the dragon seems fitting given the beast's own reputation as something of an enduring mystery. It's remarkable that just about anyone can describe what a dragon looks like and how it would likely behave without having personally seen one. But not even the fans who show up at Dragon Con, the yearly convention held in Atlanta, Georgia, that attracts more than sixty thousand lovers of fantasy, science fiction, and comic books, expect to actually see dragons other than those they find in their favorite books, movies, or television shows.

Once Thought to Be Real

Today people have many resources at their disposal for considering the true origins and meanings of dragons, among them numerous mythological tales that describe encounters between humans and dragons; scientific evidence that suggests many animals found in the wild have at least some resemblance to the mythological beasts; and a rich archive of respected literature in which highly believable descriptions of dragons are included. These resources were largely not available to people who lived hundreds of years ago when many believed that dragons were just as real as snakes and birds. As David Passes, author of the book *Dragon Legends*, states,

> Just a few hundred years ago, sightings of dragons were quite common. Ordinary people saw them; so did kings, knights, archbishops and monks. Learned scholars wrote about them. But when naturalists began their enormous

The members of the popular indie rock band Imagine Dragons came up with their name by shifting around letters in some of their favorite words. The band gained critical praise for its 2014 album Smoke + Mirrors, *which earned them a Grammy award for Best Rock Performance that year.*

task of describing and recording all the different types of animals, some people began to doubt the existence of dragons. Today, most naturalists say that dragons never existed. . . . Imagine Marco Polo in the thirteenth century, the first European to travel overland to the Far East, coming across a crocodile for the first time. His description—and an artist's rendering at the time—were exactly like a dragon.[2]

Here is the way Polo described some of the creatures he reportedly saw during his travels in Asia in his book *The Travels of Marco Polo*, originally published in 1254. Polo wrote,

> **"The nose is like a loaf of bread, the mouth so huge that it would swallow at once a man whole. The teeth are immense, nor is there any wild beast whom they do not strike with terror."[3]**
>
> *—Thirteenth-century writer and explorer Marco Polo.*

Here are snakes and serpents so huge as to strike all men with astonishment; they are ten paces long [about 48 feet or 14.8 meters], ten palms broad, and have no feet, but only a hoof like that of a lion. The nose is like a loaf of bread, the mouth so huge that it would swallow at once a man whole. The teeth are immense, nor is there any wild beast whom they do not strike with terror.[3]

Teller of Tall Tales

Moreover, in 2008 writer Mike Edwards, who studied one of Polo's later books, *The Description of the World*, and previously attempted to retrace some of Polo's steps across Asia, made this observation:

Truth to tell, many of Marco Polo's tales of treasure were just that: tales. Tall tales. Readers who persevere in Polo's often confusing, disjointed text will encounter preposterous supernatural events and an astonishing bestiary [illustrated volume of animals both real and imagined], including men with the features of dogs."[4]

Of course, Polo is no longer alive to defend his discoveries. The same is also true for many other people who have provided the basis for dragon stories that are known virtually all over the world. But there are many theories concerning which animals and indeed what natural phenomena may have led explorers and other observers to conclude that they had seen dragons. On the other hand, many people maintain that dragons have never been anything other than a myth.

Chapter 1

What Are Dragons?

"Few people today believe in the literal existence of dragons in the way they may believe in the existence of Bigfoot or the Loch Ness monster, for example. The dragon . . . is simply too big and too fantastic to take seriously or literally."

—Benjamin Radford, deputy editor of the science magazine *Skeptical Inquirer*.

Benjamin Radford, "Are Dragons Real? Facts About Dragons," LiveScience.com, December 10, 2014. www.livescience.com.

"The early medieval period was a veritable paradise for dragons. This can be attributed to the period's unusually warm temperatures and an abundance of knights, the beasts' favourite combatant and food . . . As a result, the major needs for living, feeding and, crucially, relaxation were readily available to dragons, allowing populations to flourish."

—Zoologists Andrew J. Hamilton, Robert M. May, and Edward K. Waters.

Andrew J. Hamilton, Robert M. May, and Edward K. Waters, "Here Be Dragons," *Nature*, April 2, 2015, p. 43.

Written in the thirteenth century, the *Aberdeen Bestiary* is one of the first attempts made in Western civilization to compile an encyclopedia of zoology. Historians aren't sure who wrote the *Bestiary*, only that a copy surfaced in the library of Westminster Palace in London in the 1600s.

Paging through the *Bestiary*, readers can find descriptions for all manner of animals: lions, tigers, elephants, apes, hyenas, dogs, wolves, sheep, horses, hawks, and owls, among others. All are presented with vivid descriptions of their habits, physical qualities, and diets. The *Bestiary* also includes a description of dragons, finding,

> The dragon, it is said, is often drawn forth from caves into the open air, causing the air to become turbulent.
>
> The dragon has a crest, a small mouth, and narrow blow-holes through which it breathes and puts forth its tongue. Its strength lies not in its teeth but in its tail, and it kills with a blow rather than a bite. It is free from poison. They say that it does not need poison to kill things, because it kills anything around which it wraps its tail.
>
> From the dragon not even the elephant, with its huge size, is safe. For lurking on paths along which elephants are accustomed to pass, the dragon knots its tail around their legs and kills them by suffocation.[5]

The *Bestiary* is well illustrated: The image that accompanies the description of the dragon depicts a winged orange lizard with a long tail. The head and feet of the dragon resemble those more commonly found among species of birds. Modern-day curators of the library caution readers that the thirteenth-century authors did not always rely on provable science or observation when they compiled the encyclopedia. Suggest the curators, "Although it deals with the natural world it was never meant to be a scientific text and should not be read as such. Some observations may be quite accurate but they are given the same weight as totally fabulous accounts."[6]

> **"The dragon has a crest, a small mouth, and narrow blow-holes through which it breathes and puts forth its tongue. Its strength lies not in its teeth but in its tail, and it kills with a blow rather than a bite."[5]**
>
> —Aberdeen Bestiary.

Dragons: Friends and Foes

The description and painting of the dragon that appears in the *Bestiary* is similar to other images of dragons that have emerged over the centuries. Invariably, dragons have been envisioned as huge creatures, 50 feet (15.2 m) or more from snout to tail. They are reptilian, featuring scales, a lizard's mouth and snout, and sharp teeth. Their backs are lined with razor-sharp spikes. Some are horned. Many are winged. Many breathe fire. Some can speak. Some dragons have more than one head. The English word *dragon* is believed to find its roots in the ancient Greek term *draconta*, which means monstrous worm.

In the folklore of the West, dragons are believed to have a most unpleasant demeanor. They are imagined as swooping down on unsuspecting prey, vanquishing their enemies with blasts of fiery breath, swipes of their tails, or bites from their fearsome jaws. Many dragons have been assigned to guard duty by their masters—gods, sorcerers, or kings—standing sentry before caves or atop mountains where treasures have been hidden. Unsuspecting visitors find

Although different cultures possess their own distinct vision of dragons, some basic traits tend to be shared by all. Dragons are typically large beasts with reptilian or serpentine features such as scales, long tails, and sharp teeth. Some slither like worms; others have bat-like wings that allow them to fly.

the bones of unfortunate treasure hunters scattered at the mouths of the dragons' lairs.

But thousands of miles away, the people of Asia formed far different notions about dragons. Centuries ago, Asian peoples had little or no contact with the West and yet still conjured images of dragons similar to those in the West: huge, flying reptiles capable of mystic powers. And yet there is a substantial difference between the concept of the dragon that grew in the West and that which developed in the East. In Asian folklore, dragons are often regarded as benign creatures. In the myths and religions of China and other Asian countries, dragons are revered as protectors or as guides for heroic warriors or held in high esteem for their wise counsel.

"For me, dragons are beautiful, magical creatures in any world they inhabit. They are also the most intelligent, the most powerful, and the most dangerous."[7]

—Science fiction author Margaret Weis.

This contradictory nature of the dragon—the fact that some cultures regard it as an evil beast while others believe it to be a helpful friend—is what makes it so fascinating. Says science fiction author Margaret Weis,

> For me, dragons are beautiful, magical creatures in any world they inhabit. They are also the most intelligent, the most powerful, and the most dangerous. Humans are such puny creatures compared to dragons, which can slay us with the single swipe of a claw or the whoosh of their fiery breath. Yet we dare to be drawn to dragons, whether they are evil, greedy monsters who hide in caves and guard their treasure or whether they are friendly beings who permit us to fly on their backs."[7]

Tiamat and the Creation of the Earth

Such images of dragons were well entrenched in human thought by the time the anonymous authors of the *Aberdeen Bestiary* decided to include the creatures in their encyclopedia. In fact, accounts of dragons date back to ancient times, centuries before the *Bestiary* was published. The Babylonians, who founded a civilization in 2000 BCE in a region found today in Iraq, believed the world was created from the carcass of a dragon named Tiamat. According to the myth, Tiamat was a goddess whose husband, Apsu, was slain by lesser gods. To seek revenge, Tiamat transformed herself into a dragon. "Tiamat's body was huge and serpentine, including a long, coiling trunk and a skin impervious to weapons," says Douglas Niles, a writer and authority on dragon lore. "She had a great head capped by two massive horns, with a long tail lashing from her hindquarters."[8]

Tiamat vowed to vanquish the other gods but was met in battle by Marduk, the sun god. To defeat Tiamat, Marduk summoned a hurricane. Tiamat was besieged by the fierce winds, which forced her to open her mouth. At that moment, Marduk shot an arrow into her mouth, killing Tiamat. Marduk then cut her carcass in two, using one half to shape the heavens, the other half to create the earth. Marduk was, however, not finished. After slaying Tiamat, the sun god killed her son, the god Kingu, and from the blood of Kingu, Marduk created humankind. And so, at least according to the Babylonians, the stars in the sky as well as the earth itself were created from the body of a dragon.

The Dragons of Egypt

In ancient Egypt, dragons were also regarded as powerful, mythological beasts whose existence represented a threat to the world. The mightiest of the Egyptian dragons was Apep, an enemy of Ra, the sun god. According to Egyptian myth, Apep constantly attacked Ra's boat as it sailed across the sky. Some descriptions suggest Apep stood as tall as eight men, although other stories report Apep's length spanned miles.

Apep and Ra were in continuous battle; when Ra held sway, the sun shined brightly, but as Apep gained advantage, the sun dipped below the horizon and night fell. "[Apep] thus represents the darkness of night; he also represents eclipses and thunderclouds for he may attack the sun-boat by day," says Joseph Fontenrose, a University of California at Berkeley historian. "He is constantly defeated but constantly comes back to life and tries again."[9]

The Dragon Boats

From the late eighth century to the late eleventh century, warriors from the Norse countries known as Vikings set sail on missions of conquest. They were ruthless invaders, attacking other ships as well as coastal villages. To intimidate their enemies, they carved the heads of dragons into the prows and sterns of their ships. These vessels are known as dragon barques or dragon boats. "There wasn't any place in Europe, or even the Near East, that fronted a sea or navigable river that was secure from these new barbarians who came on the backs of dragons, instead of on horseback," says Ervan Garrison, a University of Georgia anthropologist. "These 'dragons' were the Viking longships called '*drakuschiffen*' or dragon-ships because of their tall prows and sterns often carved with fierce replicas of these mythic creatures."

Dragons were a part of the myth and folklore of the Vikings. One dragon that appears prominently in Viking myth is Jormungand, a dragon so long that it could encircle the earth, taking its tail into its mouth. Another dragon is known as Fafnir. Born a human, Fafnir killed his father and made off with his treasure, hiding in a cave. He remained in the cave for many years; as his greed and selfishness grew, Fafnir lost his human qualities and turned into a dragon. Eventually, Fafnir was killed by a prince, Sigurd, who had been given a magical sword by the Norse god Odin.

Ervan G. Garrison, *A History of Engineering and Technology: Artful Methods.* Boca Raton, FL: CRC Press, 1999, p. 111.

Apep isn't the only dragon found in Egyptian myth. The Egyptians believed very strongly in dragons and wove stories about the beasts into many of their myths. For example, another evil dragon found in Egyptian mythology is Ammut, who devoured the souls of sinners. Some Egyptian dragons were revered. The dragon Mehen coiled itself around the boat of Ra and protected the sun god at night from Apep's attacks. The winged dragon laculi is believed to have guarded the tombs of the deceased. The dragon Wadjet was a symbol of royalty; images of Wadjet were engraved in the crowns of the pharaohs. The dragon Nehebkau protected the pharaohs in the afterlife.

Pliny's Dragons

In the centuries since the era of the ancient Egyptians and Babylonians, science has provided many answers that help explain the creation of the universe and the motions of the sun, and none of them include the influence of dragons. The Babylonians, Egyptians, and other ancient peoples lacked knowledge in the natural sciences, and therefore invented myths for how the earth was created, why there are stars in the sky, and why the sun sets at night and rises in the morning. But even as scholars began to acquire knowledge of the natural world, they continued to harbor beliefs that dragons were as common as elephants and whales.

> **"The Dragons are so large that they are able to receive all the Elephant's blood."[11]**
>
> *—First-century CE Roman philosopher Pliny the Elder.*

The first-century CE Roman philosopher Gaius Plinius Secundus, better known as Pliny the Elder, is regarded as one of the ancient world's most important scholars. He is the author of *Naturalis Historia*, or *Natural History*, an early encyclopedia of the natural world intended to serve as not only a reference book about zoology but also botany and geology. In it, Pliny described the habits of many living things, including dragons. Accordingly, elephants had much to fear from dragons—and vice versa. For the dragon, the elephant was desirable prey, but dragons had to be wary of elephants for they could use their girth to crush their foes. Reported Pliny:

> The Dragon . . . espying the Elephant going to its Food, throweth itself on it from a high Tree; this Creature, knowing its Inability by struggling to withstand the other's Windings about it, seeketh to crush its Enemy against the Trees or Rocks. The Dragons guard against this by entangling [elephants] first with their Tail; the Elephants undo those

> Knots with their Hand: but the Dragons put their Heads into their Snout, and so shut out their Breath, and tear the tenderest Parts. When these two chance to encounter each other on the Way, the Dragons raise themselves against their Enemies, and aim chiefly at the Eyes, whereby it happeneth that many Times they [elephants] are found blind, and worn away with Hunger and Grief.[10]

Pliny explained that dragons are mostly found in India and Ethiopia. He described their length at twenty cubits—an ancient measurement, roughly 18 inches (45.7 cm)—or about a total of thirty feet, nose to tail. "The Dragons are so large that they are able to receive all the Elephant's blood,"[11] he insisted.

Even though he had only heard tales of these fabled beasts, the first-century CE Roman natural philosopher Pliny the Elder included a description of dragons in his* Naturalis Historia*, an encyclopedia of nature. Such mixing of legend and fact kept the myth of dragons alive in Western culture.

The Pendragons

The story of the Britsh king Arthur contains many mythological elements, but historians believe the Arthurian legends are based to some degree on fact. Arthur's father was believed to be Uther Pendragon. In the Welsh language, the words *draig or ddraich* are translated into English as dragon. A *pen draig* is the chief dragon. Therefore, Uther—and his son—were regarded as leaders who were as fearsome as a dragon.

Historians suggest that Arthur ruled during the sixth century. He was preceded by many Pendragons, the first of which was Eudaf Hen, who ruled in the fourth century.

According to British historian Mike Ashley, Pendragon was a title that dated back to the Roman occupation of England. The Romans invaded England in 43 CE and remained until the early years of the fifth century. "During the Roman occupation the title must have been little more than honorific, but once the Roman yoke was lifted the Pendragon was able to re-emerge," says Ashley.

According to Arthurian legend, Uther seized the throne after his brother Aurelius was poisoned. Upon the death of Aurelius, the wizard Merlin gazed into the night sky and observed the glowing image of a dragon. Accepting the image as an omen, Merlin declared Uther a Pendragon.

Mike Ashley, *The Mammoth Book of King Arthur*. New York: Carroll & Graf, 2005, p. 173.

Moreover, Pliny suggested, it was not unusual for Roman mariners to see herds of dragons composed of four or five of the beasts flying over the Mediterranean Sea toward the countries of Arabia.

Dragons of Heraldry

There may have been as much myth as fact found in Pliny's *Naturalis Historia*, but at least the Roman scholar put some effort into the pursuit of science. Following the fall of the Roman Empire in the fifth century CE, scientific pursuit ground to a virtual halt as the Western world entered the Middle Ages, the period of history when scholarship, literature, art, and similar pursuits made little progress. Instead, kings and other rulers mostly made war, sometimes to enhance the spread of Christianity, other times simply to enrich themselves and enlarge their realms.

In many cases soldiers looked to the dragon as a symbol of courage, believing it would invoke fear in their enemies. And so illustrations of dragons were etched onto their shields or embroidered onto their tunics. Dragons were also incorporated into the coats of arms of many royal houses.

> "The dragon is one of the most artistic of heraldic creations, and lends itself very readily to the genius of any artist."[12]
>
> *—Heraldry expert Arthur Charles Fox-Davies.*

The designs and symbols in a coat of arms were considered a serious matter in the Middle Ages. Nobles did not take these designs lightly. In fact, the design of these emblems belongs to an art form known as heraldry. Arthur Charles Fox-Davies, an expert on heraldry, explains the significance of a dragon found in a coat of arms:

> The head of a dragon is like nothing else in heraldry, and from what source it originated or what basis existed for ancient heraldic artists to imagine it must remain a mystery, unless it has developed from the crocodile or from some antediluvian animal much akin. It is like nothing else in heaven or on earth. Its neck is covered with scales not unlike those of a fish. All four legs are scaled and have claws, the back is scaled, the tongue is barbed, and the under part of the body is likewise scaled, but here, in rolls of a much larger size. Great differences will be found in the shape of the ears, but the wings of the dragon are always represented as the wings of a bat, with the long ribs or bones carried to the base. The dragon is one of the most artistic of heraldic creations, and lends itself very readily to the genius of any artist.[12]

Differing Tastes in Dragons

According to Fox-Davies, various kings and nobles of the era adopted different styles of dragons to their coats of arms, evidently to meet personal tastes. In England, he says, monarchs from the House of Tudor preferred dragons with smooth tails while other nobles preferred to add barbs to the ends of the dragons' tails. Moreover, the Tudor kings of England, including Henry VII, Henry VIII, and Edward VI, preferred red dragons. But the Tudor queen Elizabeth I changed the color of the royal dragon to gold. Welsh nobles also preferred red dragons. In the heraldry of German nobles, dragons were usually depicted on four feet.

The posture of the dragon was given considerable attention by the artists, each stance having a particular name. A *rampant* dragon was depicted raising one claw above the other as if to make a motion to attack. The *passant* dragon stood on three legs with one front leg lifted as though in mid-stride. The *statant* dragon stood on all four feet in sharp attention. The *couchant* dragon was drawn in a relaxed pose, its four legs folded beneath it, but with a raised head, showing it to be alert, perhaps in anticipation of danger.

There are various mythical creatures found in heraldry that resemble dragons. Among them is the wyvern, which has the head, body, wings, and tail of a dragon but stands on two legs rather than four. The four-legged dragon is common to heraldry. There is also the cockatrice, which has the body, wings, and tail of a dragon but the head of a rooster, which gives it less of a reptilian appearance, meaning it also lacks the classic look of the dragon.

Dragons of China

While the European concept of a dragon holds that the beasts are fearsome and evil creatures, that is not the case in Asian cultures. A number of Asian peoples have formulated their own beliefs about dragons, which run counter to the notion that dragons are maleficent beings. In China, for example, ancient emperors believed themselves to be descended from dragons, known in

Though it shares some of the fearsome features of its European counterpart, the Chinese dragon is a symbol of power and good fortune. The dragon was the emblem of early Chinese emperors who were thought to have shared their lineage with these strong and wise beasts.

the Chinese language as *lung*. Outwardly, Asian dragons resemble those of European culture: they are envisioned as large reptilian animals that possess mythical powers. Inwardly though, many Asian cultures believed the role of a dragon to be a benign, spiritual guide. Says Niles, "The dragons, or *lung*, of the Chinese mythos were universally powerful, long-lived, and wise beings."[13]

Among the benign dragons revered in Chinese culture is Tien-lung, who was tasked with guarding the palace of the gods. One story finds Tien-lung descending from the heavens to gaze upon a painting rendered by an artist. Although Tien-lung gazed admiringly, the dragon's presence frightened the artist away.

Many other dragons appear in Chinese mythology, each assigned specific tasks or characteristics. Shen-lung was revered by farmers because the dragon was believed to control the weather. For this reason, asking Shen-lung for rain or sunshine became a ritual among ancient Chinese farmers. Shen-lung was also believed to have a playful nature: the dragon was regarded as lazy and often shirked its responsibilities by shrinking to the size of a mouse and hiding in a haystack or thatched roof, or even in the house of a farmer. The dragon Ti-lung watched over rivers, lakes, and streams. Futs-lung guarded the Chinese underworld; specifically tasked with protecting precious metals and jewels. These dragons and others from Chinese myth possessed many powers, among them the gifts of speech and writing. Chinese dragons were said to have the power to use their tails to dig new channels into rivers, assisting sailors. Many dragons were said to bestow gifts upon people, mainly pearls and other jewels.

Dragons of Korea, Japan, and India

In addition to the Chinese, other Asian peoples who have harbored beliefs in dragons include Filipinos, Indians, Indonesians, Japanese, Koreans, Malaysians, and Vietnamese. As with the Chinese, the Koreans look to dragons for spiritual guidance; Korean dragons are often depicted wearing long beards, giving them the appearance of wise and elderly creatures. In Eastern cultures, elderly people—and elderly dragons—are believed to possess the most wisdom. "The dragons of Korea are generally viewed as benign and helpful creatures and have a great deal of influence over water," says Niles. "They are credited with causing rain, and many tales refer to dragons living in rivers and lakes, shallow seas, and even small ponds in the mountains or in freshwater springs."[14]

As with the Chinese, the ancient Japanese people believed their rulers were also descended from dragons. According to ancient Japanese beliefs, the dragon Ryujin (the name translates to "luminous being") had a huge mouth and could swallow ships whole. Ryujin's scales, claws, horns, and tongue were blue. It is said that Ryujin's daughter, the goddess Otohime, mated with a human, the hunter Hoori. Their son—the grandson of a dragon—was Jimmu Tenno, the first emperor of Japan.

Dragons also appear in ancient stories in Hinduism, the dominant religion of India. Known as nāgas, the dragons are believed to be descended from the Hindu gods Kadru and Kasyapa.

Nāgas are believed to possess many powers, including the power to change into human form. The bite of a nāga could be fatal, but nāgas are admonished by the god Brahma to bite evil people only. However, the nāgas are also known to bite those with fatal diseases or injuries as a way to painlessly hasten their deaths.

Lacking Scientific Proof

Regardless of how dragons are depicted in the literature and art of the world's cultures, dragons remain no more than a myth. Although there have been many stories written and told about dragons, not a single eyewitness account of a dragon encounter has held up to serious scientific scrutiny. Photographs purported to have captured images of dragons have been thoroughly debunked as fakes. Says Benjamin Radford, deputy editor of the science magazine *Skeptical Inquirer*, "In the modern age of satellite imagery and smart phone photos and videos, it's simply implausible that any giant, unknown winged fire-breathers inhabit Earth's skies unseen."[15] Indeed, even the Loch Ness Monster or Bigfoot have prompted scientific inquiry due to many photos, videos, and eyewitness accounts—but that hasn't been the case with dragons.

A typical "dragon sighting" occurred in 2014 when a Malaysian man claimed to have killed a *naga putih*—Malay for white dragon. According to news reports, he found a thin white creature, some thirty feet in length, crawling across the floor in his home. The creature had the body of a snake, yet it also had four short legs and four clawed feet. Its head resembled the classic image of a dragon's head featuring a long snout, razor-sharp teeth, and horns. A story published in the Malaysian media reported,

> A dragon was shot dead at a house near a durian [a type of fruit] orchard when its owner realized that he has been losing a few of his pet rabbits as of late. The durian orchard owner, Boon Chin Yo, was sleeping in the 2-storey house when he was suddenly awoken by a rabbit's screams and a weird noise, much like a tiger. He peeped from the stairs only to find a strange animal with horns and long whiskers

> attacking a rabbit. Out of panic, he quickly made a grab for his auto rifle and shot at it 8 times, causing the strange animal to fall onto the floor. After ensuring that it was really dead, he was shocked to find that it was a white dragon with fur like a rabbit. When met with reporters, he said, "I wouldn't have guessed that it'd turn out to be a white dragon. It shocked me."[16]

Internet snoops soon unearthed other pictures of the "white dragon," finding images that revealed the creature was actually made of clay and had been fashioned in an artist's workshop before the trickster photographed the "carcass" in his home. Conceded one Asian news outlet that reported the story, "We were duped and are willing to hold our hands up when we are wrong. It was a bloody good fake though."[17]

Adventure, Thrills, and Danger

Still, some scientists are willing to give dragons the benefit of the doubt. They concede there is no hard evidence, such as fossils or legitimate photographs, to suggest dragons exist today or even centuries ago. Nevertheless, they argue that many elements of folklore have at least some basis in fact. In a 2015 issue of the scientific journal *Nature*, zoologists Andrew J. Hamilton, Robert M. May, and Edward K. Waters asked, "What if the legends were rooted in truth? The differences in appearance—some lack wings, some have multiple heads and some seem not to breathe fire—once thought to reflect local traditions, can also be readily explained by [the difference in species]."[18]

Whether dragons truly did exist or whether dragons are merely the invention of ancient and medieval storytellers, there is no question that dragons have continued to enthrall people well into the twenty-first century. Regardless of whether the creature is looked upon as good or evil, stories about dragons have always delivered a measure of adventure, thrills, and danger.

Chapter 2

Encounters with Dragons

"The Dragon is the terrific oppressor, assailing with teeth and claws, armed all over with spikes, lifting speary [sharp and pointed] wings and tail, spouting fire and fury, and rushing upon its prey with every vehemence of malignant energy."

—Theologian Joseph Seiss.

Joseph Seiss, *The Gospel in the Stars*. New York: Cosimo, 2007, p. 58.

"From prehistoric days until [ancient Greece] there is no evidence to show that the dragon was inimical to the gods or malevolent towards mankind. It inspired awe because it possessed supernatural qualities."

—Archaeologist Elizabeth Douglas Van Buren.

Quoted in James H. Charlesworth, *The Good and Evil Serpent: How a Universal Symbol Became Christianized.* New Haven, CT: Yale University Press, 2012, p. 62.

Encounters with dragons can be found in folklore, fairy tales, mythology, classic and modern literature, and in books of the Bible. In Western civilization, dragons are portrayed as evil and loathsome creatures possessing superior strength and magical powers. Invariably, the heroes who encounter, and defeat, dragons are portrayed as fearless, strong, and noble. Battles between heroes and dragons are often framed as struggles between good and evil.

In Asian mythology and folklore, though, dragons are more likely to be on the side of goodness. Many Asian stories involving dragons feature battles between good and evil, but in Asian myth, dragons often provide wise counsel and guidance that helps the hero defeat the villain.

The Hydra of Lerna

In Western mythology, perhaps no champion exemplified the attributes of strength and courage as much as the Greek hero Heracles, known in Roman mythology as Hercules. According to Greek myth, Heracles battled a dragon known as the Hydra of Lerna. The Hydra was itself the offspring of two monstrous creatures: Typhon and Echidna. Typhon was said to have 100 heads—including some heads that sprouted from his fingers. Echidna was half human, half snake. The Hydra dwelled in the marshes of Lerna, a region in southern Greece, guarding a cave that led to the underworld. Whenever unsuspecting humans or livestock wandered too close to the cave entrance, the Hydra emerged and devoured the hapless victims. Even the breath of the Hydra could be deadly—it was said the Hydra exhaled poisonous vapors.

The Hydra also had many heads—all but one of them immortal. When one of the Hydra's heads was cut off, it would be replaced by two more heads. These immortal heads surrounded and guarded the mortal head of the Hydra. Says Robert Graves, a scholar of Greek mythology, "The Hydra had a prodigious dog-like body, and eight or nine snaky heads . . . but some credit it with fifty, or one hundred, or even ten thousand heads. In all events it was so venomous that its very breath, or the smell of its tracks, could destroy life."[19] The only way to kill the Hydra, then, was to fight through its immortal protectors and cut off the beast's mortal head.

The Labors of Heracles

The slaying of the Hydra was one of twelve labors assigned to Heracles by King Thespius so that Heracles could atone for the crime of murdering his six children. (Heracles committed the murders after being driven to insanity by the goddess Hera.) Many of these labors involved killing or capturing fantastic beasts, among them the Nemean lion, the Erymanthian boar, the man-eating Stymphalian birds, and the Cretan bull.

To slay the Hydra, Heracles enlisted the aid of his nephew Iolaus. Arriving in Lerna, the two heroes lit torches and approached the Hydra's lair slowly. They held the torches close to the cave entrance so that smoke would enter the cavern, flushing the beast from its lair. Says Karl Shuker, a zoologist and expert on dragons,

> The two men backed away, coughing and wiping their streaming eyes; and when they looked back, they beheld a sight so dreadful that even [Heracles'] fiery blood ran cold in his veins. The acrid smoke had dispelled, exposing a vast, bloated mass of pulsating flesh, obscenely corpulent and of a sickening pallid hue.

The Greek demigod Heracles battled the dragon-like Lernaean Hydra as one of his famous twelve labors. The Hydra had one massive body with nine reptilian heads atop long, serpentine necks. When Heracles chopped off one head, he was surprised to see that two more grew in its place.

> Superficially, it resembled a grotesque octopus or squid, for above this obese sac of a body thrashed a flailing mass of tentacle-like appendages—but that was where any such similarity abruptly ended. For as [Heracles] and Iolaus could see only too clearly, these "tentacles" were, in fact, nine powerful necks, and each of the necks terminated in an evil, horned head, the head of a dragon.[20]

> "Superficially, [the Hydra] resembled a grotesque octopus or squid, for above this obese sac of a body thrashed a flailing mass of tentacle-like appendages—but that was where any such similarity abruptly ended."[20]
>
> *—Karl Shuker, zoologist and expert on dragons.*

Mindful of the Hydra's poisonous breath, Heracles and Iolaus covered their mouths with cloths so they would not breathe in the deadly vapors. Heracles and Iolaus then lit the heads of arrows. Heracles drew his bow and fired the arrows at the Hydra. The attack prompted the Hydra to lunge at Heracles. As the dragon approached, Heracles dropped his bow and drew his sword. He lopped off a head but the Hydra's missing head was quickly replaced by two more heads. Heracles swung his sword and cut off a second head, but again two living heads grew in place on the stump of the Hydra's neck.

Death of the Hydra

Realizing this strategy to be futile, Heracles and Iolaus withdrew from the lair and made camp nearby where they hoped to devise a new plan to kill the Hydra. Iolaus suggested that he would accompany Heracles to the lair of the Hydra carrying a flaming torch in hand. As soon as Heracles lopped off the head of the beast, Iolaus would touch the flame to the stump, immediately cauterizing, or sealing, the wound so new heads would not grow in its place. "I'll sear the wound after you cut off the head,"[21] he said.

Heracles and Iolaus approached the lair of the Hydra and again used smoke to flush the dragon from its cave. Heracles struck again, slicing a head from the Hydra's body. This time, Iolaus acted quickly, searing the wound. As they expected, no new

The Story of Draco the Dragon

In addition to the battle of Heracles and the Hydra, Greek mythology records a second encounter between Heracles and a dragon. This encounter occurred at the Garden of Hesperides, located in what historians believe are the Canary Islands, off the Atlantic coast of Africa. It was there that Heracles fought a dragon known as the Ladon.

Like the Hydra, the Ladon is said to have had many heads—as many as 100, with each head capable of speech. Also, each mouth was lined with razor-sharp teeth, making the Ladon capable of tearing limbs from intruders. The Ladon's body was long and serpentine, able to crush the life out of an enemy. The Ladon also used its tail, which was long and powerful, to strike an enemy, smashing his bones.

The Ladon never slept, which made the dragon ideal for the task assigned to it by the goddess Hera: guarding a tree that sprouted apples made of gold. The Ladon guarded the tree by coiling its body around the trunk, its 100 heads constantly looking in all directions for intruders. Heracles slew the dragon by firing poison-tipped arrows into the body of the beast. Heracles then helped himself to the golden apples.

But the story of the Ladon lives on. According to myth, Hera cast the body of the dragon into the sky, where it assumed its place among the stars. Modern-day observers can look toward Polaris, the North Star, to find a constellation known as Draco, the Dragon.

heads grew in its place. They used this strategy several times—chopping and searing—until the last head remained.

Heracles made one final strike with his sword, slicing the last head from the Hydra's body. It was the mortal head, for no new heads grew in its place. Even as the last living head tumbled to the ground, it continued to hiss and snarl. Heracles lifted the head and tossed it into a deep hole, then covered the hole with dirt and rocks.

Beowulf and the Dragon

In the epic poem *Beowulf*, the hero Beowulf exemplifies the same attributes as Heracles. He is courageous, a leader of men, and vanquished an evil enemy who terrorized his people: the giant Grendel. Written sometime between the sixth and tenth centuries by an anonymous Anglo-Saxon author, *Beowulf* is believed to be the oldest known example of verse written in English. The poem spans more than 3,000 lines.

In the Anglo-Saxon poem* Beowulf*, the elder Norse king of that name fought a dragon that terrorized his land. The hallmarks of that beast are still shared by the popular notion of the dragon in Western culture today. For example, the dragon in* Beowulf *lived in a cave, guarded a treasure, and breathed fire.

The events of the poem take place in the Norse countries and specifically, the kingdom of Geatland, found in modern-day southern Sweden. As a young warrior, Beowulf defeated the evil Grendel and was elevated to king by the Geats. He ruled for fifty years, but then Geatland fell under a new attack by a dragon, which was angered when a thief stole a golden goblet from the monster's lair.

The dragon woke to discover the missing goblet and left its lair, wreaking havoc upon the farms and villages of Geatland. In the poem, the dragon is described as some 50 feet (15.2 m) in length. It has lived for at least three hundred years—the period the poet suggests the dragon has guarded its treasure. The dragon's lair is located inside a dark cave. It has the ability to fly and spew fire from its mouth. It attacks only at night, catching its victims when they are most helpless. Reads the poem, "The old twilight-scather found the joy-bringing hoard standing open, the naked, hateful, fiery dragon, which seeketh the (grave)-mounds, and flieth by night encompassed by fire; him dwellers upon earth fear exceedingly."[22]

Beowulf realized he would have to vanquish the dragon in battle, but now the elderly king knew he would need help and called on the warriors of Geatland to assist him. Eleven knights accompanied him to the lair of the dragon.

Wiglaf Stands by His King

In the poem, Beowulf approached the cave of the dragon, commanding the beast to emerge. Suddenly, a great blast of fire spewed forth from the cave opening. The fire engulfed Beowulf, who was protected by his armor and shield; nevertheless, he sustained injuries from the flames. Upon seeing the blast of fire, though, ten of Beowulf's warriors ran away. According to the poem:

> No faithful Comrades
> Crowded about him, his chosen band,
> Fled to the wood. One of them only,
> Felt surging sorrow; for nought can stifle
> Call of a kin in a comrade true;
> Wiglaf his name . . . [23]

The lone warrior to remain at Beowulf's side was Wiglaf, the son of a knight who years before fought alongside Beowulf. Together Beowulf and Wiglaf drew their swords and slashed at the dragon, finally chopping off its head. Although the two warriors slew the dragon, Beowulf sustained mortal wounds and died as well. His death is described in the poem:

> The beast,
> guardian of the hoard hidden there,
> got nothing from the battle
> but death.
>
> The dragon
> slew one man,
> only one,
> all the blood needed to work out fate's plan.
>
> The scene of a warrior's
> last stand remains
> a mystery. He never knows
> if after the battle
> he'll sit drinking mead
> with friends again.
>
> So it was with Beowulf,
> death made that mission his last.[24]

Beowulf is a classic story of good versus evil, but in the poem, good doesn't necessarily triumph. The refusal of the Geat warriors to help their king defeat the dragon led to the death of Beowulf, a most noble hero. At the conclusion of the fight, the cowardly warriors gathered around the body of Beowulf. Wiglaf scolded them for abandoning their king in what should have been for them a time to show their courage. And he warned them that without Beowulf to lead them, the Geats would face grave danger from their enemies. Wiglaf's prophecies came true, and the Geats were soon attacked by foreign invaders. According to poets Michael Spring and Lewis Warsh, the battle against the dragon—a source of evil—would have helped unite the knights of Geat and made them into stronger and more courageous warriors. By failing to rise to the challenge posed by the dragon, the knights exposed themselves as cowards and weaklings. "The most important bond in Anglo-Saxon society was the relation between king and warrior," say Spring and Warsh. "When the Geat warriors break the bond by refusing to assist Beowulf in his battle against the dragon, the foundation of society collapses, and chaos rules."[25]

"When the Geat warriors break the bond by refusing to assist Beowulf in his battle against the dragon, the foundation of society collapses, and chaos rules."[25]

—Poets Michael Spring and Lewis Warsh.

St. George and the Dragon

The poet who wrote *Beowulf* was likely to have been inspired by stories from the Christian Bible. The Bible contains many references to dragons, all portrayed as maleficent and evil. "In biblical . . . texts, the dragon features as one of the commonest Christian symbols of evil, functioning as a formidable and monstrous adversary of God, man and beast alike,"[26] says Christine Rauer, a professor of English at the University of St. Andrews in Scotland.

In the Book of Revelation 20:1, Satan, the ultimate embodiment of evil, is described as a dragon:

> Then I saw an angel coming down from heaven, holding in his hand the key to the bottomless pit and a great chain. And he seized the dragon, that ancient serpent, who is the devil and Satan, and bound him for a thousand years, and threw him into the pit, and shut it and sealed it over him, so that he might not deceive the nations any longer, until the thousand years were ended.

Perhaps the most familiar story of a Christian hero battling a dragon is that of St. George. The story concerns a warrior of the Roman Empire, said to have been born in Turkey in the third century. At the time, much of the civilized world was still ruled by the Romans, who persecuted Christians. George, a soldier in the service of the emperor Diocletian, was undeterred by the persecution and openly practiced his faith. But when Diocletian decreed that all Christians would be put to death, George fled the Roman army and resolved to roam the land on horseback, spreading his faith.

Arriving in the Libyan city of Silene, George learned that a terrible dragon dwelled at a lakeside. At first, the dragon preyed on the cattle and sheep kept by the Silenese people. When the dragon devoured a young shepherd, the Silenese king declared he had no choice but to make a peace offering to the monster—the sacrifice of a sheep left for the dragon each morning. When the dragon had devoured all the sheep in the city, the king decided to offer children as sacrifices to the creature. And so each morning a child was chosen by lottery. The unfortunate victim was tied to a rock by the lake and devoured by the dragon. After many children died, the king's daughter Elisaba was chosen in the lottery. The king offered his fortune to any family that would substitute their child for the princess, but the Silenese people, angered that they had lost so many of their own children, refused the pleas of the king. And so the next morning the princess, dressed in a bridal gown, was taken to the lakeside and tied to the rock to await her fate.

> "In biblical . . . texts, the dragon features as one of the commonest Christian symbols of evil, functioning as a formidable and monstrous adversary of God, man and beast alike."[26]
>
> —*Christine Rauer, professor of English at the University of St. Andrews in Scotland.*

Vanquishing the Dragon

It was then that George arrived at the lakeside atop his white horse, discovering the princess tied to the rock. He untied Elisaba, but the princess begged him to pass, telling him of the dragon and warning him that he too would become a victim of the beast. Instead, George resolved to fight the dragon.

Suddenly the dragon appeared. "It was a huge, flame-breathing dragon,"[27] says historian Joseph Fontenrose. George quickly made the sign of the cross, raised his lance, and charged. His lance pierced the mouth of the dragon, but the wound was not mortal. As the dragon thrashed about on the ground, George asked the princess for her belt. He then wrapped the belt around the neck of the dragon, using it to lash the beast to his horse.

George hoisted Elisaba onto his horse. They returned to Silene, dragging the dragon behind. Upon arriving in the city, the Silenese

In Christian myths, the dragon was an evil that only the righteous could vanquish. However, the tale of St. George slaying the fearsome dragon of Silene not only recounts the defeat of evil but the spreading of faith, for George only accepted the risk once the Silenese agreed to become Christians.

people begged George to leave, fearing the dragon would regain its strength. George, seizing the opportunity to spread the Christian faith, promised the Silenese people he would slay the dragon if they accepted Christ as their savior. The Silenese people agreed, and George chopped off the dragon's head.

Patron Saint of Great Britain

The tale of St. George is one of the most revered in Christianity, for it tells the story of a persecuted Christian who is able to show heroism in the face of a terrible enemy. And in doing so, he proved the existence of the Christian god by making the sign of the cross before attacking the dragon; therefore, his lance was guided by the Lord. Moreover, his feat convinced nonbelievers—the pagans of Silene—to accept Christianity.

Fontenrose suggests that the story of St. George reflects the epitome of the theme of good versus evil, for it is really more about the Lord defeating Satan than about a mortal conquering a large reptilian beast. "It was the Lord who sent him to the afflicted country, that by killing the dragon he might convert the king and the people,"[28] says Fontenrose.

Moreover, following the slaying of the dragon, the Silenese king offered to shower George with riches, but George insisted that the treasure be distributed among the poor. Therefore, in this case, by slaying the dragon, George did not win the prize of the dragon's treasure but the treasure of a pagan king—which he gave to charity. For these deeds, in the fifth century Pope Gelasius I canonized George, making him a saint. Today, the British people celebrate George as the patron saint of their land. Throughout Great Britain, April 23 is celebrated as St. George's Day. Moreover, George is revered as the patron saint of flocks and herds, protecting the source of milk for the British people. He is also said to ward off wolves and act as the protector of crops.

The Dragon of Mango Pond

As the stories of St. George, Beowulf, and Heracles illustrate, dragons in the folklore and religion of Western civilization invari-

Gaoliang and the Dragons

Not all dragons portrayed in Asian folklore are wise and good. One story of evil dragons is tied to the founding of the Chinese capital of Beijing. According to the myth, in the fourteenth century the emperor decided to build a new city in swampland that happened to be the home of a clan of dragons. The dragons were happy in their swamp and didn't want humans as neighbors.

A crew of builders arrived to erect the city. To put a stop to it, the head dragon and his mate changed themselves into an elderly man and woman, then placed two jars of water into a pushcart and made their way to the palace. They asked the emperor for permission to take the jars into the hills. The emperor granted them permission, not realizing the crafty dragons had magically stolen all the city's fresh water and had stored it in the jugs.

The next day the city's residents found themselves without any water. Realizing he had been tricked, the emperor sent a warrior, Gaoliang, to search for the man and woman. When he found them, they changed back into dragons and hurled one of the jugs at Gaoliang. A great torrent of water followed Gaoliang as he raced back to the city. He did not make it—as he reached the gates he was overcome by the flood and drowned. To honor the warrior who returned water to the city, a Beijing bridge is named the Gaoliang Bridge.

ably stood for evil and were faced by heroes who called on their courage, skills as warriors, and faith in God to vanquish the monsters. But that is not always the case in the folklore of the Asian world. Although there are stories of maleficent dragons in the culture of the East, most stories about dragons portray them as taking the side of good.

The story of the dragon of Mango Pond serves as an example. Mango Pond is a lake in Japan that, folklore suggests, was once inhabited by a dragon that drew all its powers from the water. Occasionally, though, the dragon enjoyed the sunshine and ventured onto dry land. First, as was its habit, the dragon changed itself into a snake, then slithered onto the shore to enjoy the warmth of the sun's rays.

One day while the dragon was warming itself, a *tengu*—a mythological creature said to be a combination of a bird, dog, and human—spotted the snake and swooped down, catching it in its talons. The tengu tried to crush the snake to death, as it had done with other snakes, but found it could not kill this particular snake (probably because the snake was really a dragon).

The Dragon Regains Its Powers

Frustrated with its failure to kill the snake, the tengu decided instead to fly the snake back to its lair atop a mountain and deal with it later. During the flight, the blowing air dried the snake, robbing the dragon of its powers. Therefore, the snake could not turn back into its real form and was helpless against the tengu. Finally, the tengu arrived at its lair and stuffed the snake into a cave on the mountainside, then sealed the cave with a rock.

Sometime later the tengu returned, removed the rock and deposited another prisoner—a monk—into the cave. After sealing the cave again, the tengu departed. The snake then surprised the monk by speaking, asking the monk how he came to be captured by the tengu. "I was fetching water from the stream," the monk said, "And just as I rose to return to my home that creature swooped down and snatched me." The monk then showed the snake the jug of water. "If you pour that water upon me my powers will be restored and I will be able to fly us out of here and back to safety,"[29] said the snake. The monk shrugged and did as the snake asked him. As the snake promised, it immediately began to change form. Within seconds the snake assumed its true form as a dragon and easily pushed the rock aside that blocked the entrance to the cave.

Both Good and Evil

The dragon flew the monk back to his home. When the monk asked the dragon if it intended to return to Mango Pond, the dragon said he planned on making his way home, but first he had some business to settle with a tengu.

Although the dragon of Mango Pond was by no means an evil creature, it was still a character in a story that pitted the forces of good against the forces of evil. In this case, the dragon teamed with a monk—a human and certainly a symbol of goodness and piety—to thwart the intentions of the tengu, a decidedly evil creature. And so the dragon has found its place in the myths of human civilization. Sometimes it is represented as a force of pure evil, other times as a kindly creature, simply minding its own business, enjoying the sunshine, meaning no one any harm.

Chapter 3

The Science of Dragons

"Granted, not all legends are based on fossils, but I'm pretty convinced some are."

—Peter Dodson, professor of veterinary anatomy, University of Pennsylvania.

Quoted in John Roach, "Dino-Era Fossils Inspired Monster Myths, Author Says," *National Geographic*, June 17, 2005. http://news.nationalgeographic.com.

"If dragons in fact were entirely mythological, if they were a figment of the imagination, and if they never ever did exist, then God just compared our adversary to a make-believe creature that never existed."

—Darek Isaacs, creationist author.

—Quoted in Meredith Bennett-Smith, "Creationist Darek Isaacs Calls Dragons Real, Says They Lived in Biblical Times," *Huffington Post*, August 15, 2013. www.huffingtonpost.com.

On a warm day in the spring of 2003, a small group of amateur fossil hunters stumbled upon a fascinating discovery while exploring an area known as the Hell Creek Formation in South Dakota. Despite being in a well-traveled location for fossil hunters, brothers Patrick and Steve Saulsbury and their friend Brian Buckmeier spotted a large skull. The skull was fairly intact, and its age was later estimated at sixty-six million years. Patrick Saulsbury remembers the drama of the moment: "Suddenly, Brian rounded a bend running full out at us yelling, 'Skull! Skull! Skull!' Steve and I raced back with him to the site. There we found an amazing ventral portion of a maxilla [upper jaw] with teeth and several node-like osteoderms [bony deposits that served as armor]."[30]

Even though they were excited, the amateur paleontologists (scientists who study fossils) didn't know exactly what they had found until they donated the skull to the Children's Museum of Indianapolis. Museum paleontologists soon declared that the Saulsburys and Buckmeier had discovered the skull of a previously unknown species of dinosaur. The museum next formed a committee that included hundreds of children as well as J.K. Rowling, the British author of the Harry Potter series of books, and asked the group to give the new dinosaur a scientific name.

The committee named the dinosaur *Dracorex hogwartsia*, in honor of the school attended by fictional boy wizard Harry as well as the skull's dragon-like appearance. In fact, when the skull was shown to the public for the first time, Paul Saulsbury witnessed a child's amazed reaction. He recalls, "One boy who was just beaming came up to Brian, Steve, and me [and said], 'I just knew there were dragons!'"[31]

This computerized image shows the proposed skeleton of* Dracorex hogwartsia*, a newly discovered dinosaur, based on unusual skull fragments found in 2003. The bony knobs on the skull resemble horns, and these may have convinced ancient fossil finders that they had uncovered the bones of dragons.

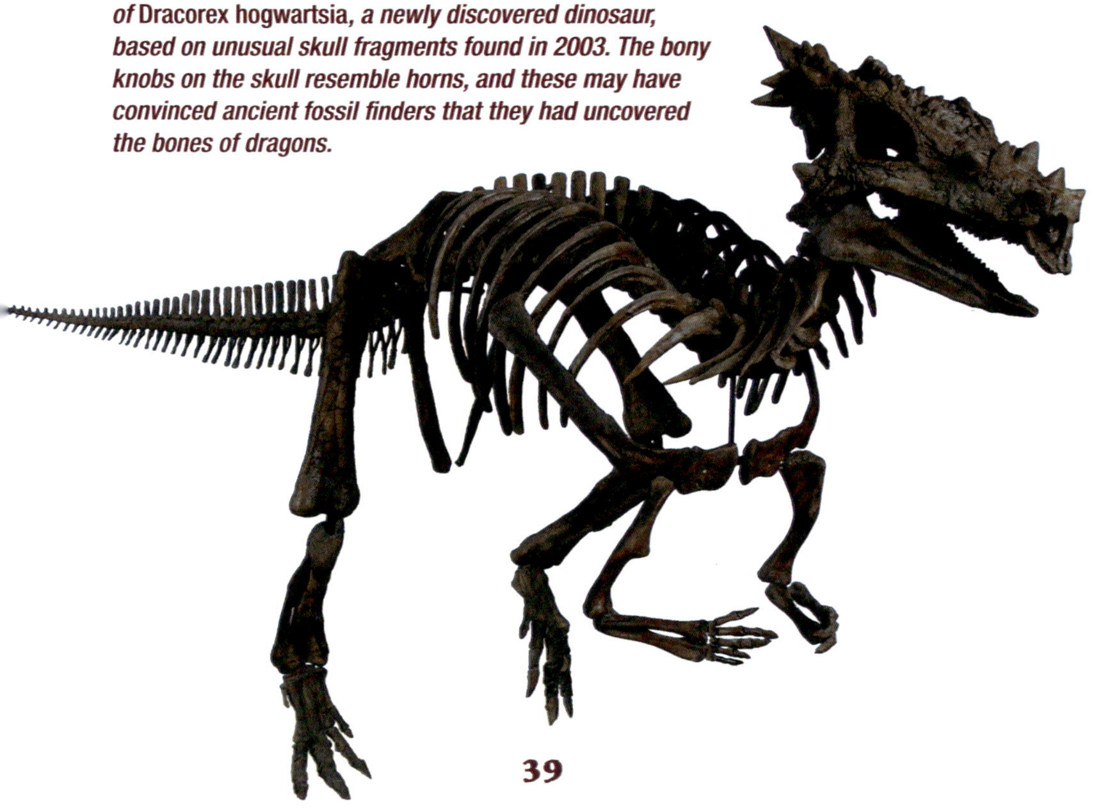

Fossils Inspired Legends

The boy's reaction made complete sense to Adrienne Mayor, a visiting scholar from Stanford University near Palo Alto, California. Mayor specializes in examining the link between classic literature, myths, and scientific history. To her, the dinosaur-dragon connection was inescapable. She says, "The shape of the dinosaur's skull, with its long muzzle, bizarre knobs and horns, surprised the scientists. But the skull looks strangely familiar to anyone who has studied dragons! *Dracorex* has a remarkable resemblance to the dragons of ancient China and medieval Europe."[32]

> "*Dracorex* helps us understand how fossils of mysterious, extinct animals may have inspired ancient people around the world to believe that dragons and other fabulous creatures once lived. Like modern paleontologists, fossil hunters in antiquity tried to imagine the appearance and behavior of the creatures whose bones they found."[33]
>
> —*Stanford University professor Adrienne Mayor.*

Finding a fossil such as *Dracorex* provides a window for modern humans to understand what finders of ancient fossils might have been thinking when they found strange bones, notes Mayor. She says, "*Dracorex* helps us understand how fossils of mysterious, extinct animals may have inspired ancient people around the world to believe that dragons and other fabulous creatures once lived. Like modern paleontologists, fossil hunters in antiquity tried to imagine the appearance and behavior of the creatures whose bones they found."[33]

She is convinced that Sioux Indians who once lived where *Dracorex* was found based their legend of the horned water serpent Unktehi on its bones. According to the legend, the evil water spirit caused a flood to kill the other creatures that lived with him. His enemies were giant birds whose beating wings made the sound of thunder and whose eyes flashed lightning. Known as Wakinyan, the thunder birds engaged in a lengthy battle lasting years until they were finally able to kill the Unktehi.

The Dragon of Klagenfurt

Australian paleontologist Othenio Abel, writing in 1914, concluded that the peoples of ancient civilizations might have been fooled

Dragons Could Never Fly

In popular culture as well as ancient mythology, dragons are winged animals often depicted in flight. However, biologists have looked at the bodies of dragons and have determined that, given their girth, they could never become airborne.

According to Peter Hogarth, a professor of biology at the University of York in Great Britain, the wingspan of a giant reptilian dragon would have to be enormous to meet the laws of physics that apply to birds and aircraft. He says, "There are certain laws of physics you can't quite get round. If it's an animal that's flying, there's a certain relationship between the wing area and the mass. The bigger the mass, the bigger the wing area, and with very large animals there's not enough room on the animal for big-enough wings."

In addition, Hogarth says, the dragon would have to be incredibly powerful to flap its wings with the rapid motion it would take to defy gravity. "[Flying] requires a lot of muscle," he says.

Quoted in Owen Williams, "Could Dragons Exist? We Ask An Expert," *Empire*, December 20, 2013. www.empireonline.com.

into believing in dragons after finding the skulls of gigantic cave bears that had lived in what is now Europe during the Ice Age. The huge bears sometimes weighed more than 2,000 pounds and ironically were not meat eaters. Nevertheless their bones were used for medicinal purposes and were believed by the ancient peoples to be dragon bones.

Abel also determined that a statue dating back to 1636, erected in the town square of Klagenfurt, Austria, was probably based on a dinosaur fossil. The statue depicts the Greek mythological hero Heracles battling a dragon. (Work on the statue was started in 1590 by sculptor Ulrich Vogelsang, who died before its completion. An unknown artist completed the statute.) According to Abel, the head of the dragon was based on a skull unearthed near Klagenfurt in 1355 and displayed in the Klagenfurt city hall. Abel determined the skull is that of a *Coelodonta*, a prehistoric rhinoceros. In fairness to Vogelsang and the unknown artist who completed the statue, the *Coelodonta* skull did feature at least one dragon-like quality: two massive horns jutted out from the beast's nasal region.

Still, lacking knowledge of paleontology—not until the seventeenth century would the British naturalist Robert Hooke first suggest the existence of extinct species—the people of the 1500s were more than willing to accept the reality of dragons. This meant that anyone who observed the old rhino skull sitting in the Klagenfurt city hall was likely to walk outside, view Vogelsang's dragon, and make a connection between the two. In fact, belief in dragons over science would endure for hundreds of years. In 1734 Swedish naturalist Carl Linnaeus observed the bones of what had been touted as a seven-headed Hydra on display in the German city of Hamburg. Linnaeus concluded it was nothing less than a fake and had been fabricated from assorted animal bones. The local merchants who bought the Hydra bones from a German count for a substantial sum of gold were so angered by Linnaeus's assertion that they drove him out of town after threatening to sue him. Says Peter J. Hogarth, a biologist at the University of York in Great Britain, "The new zoology had lost a first skirmish with the old."[34]

The Relationship of Dragons to Living Creatures

While the discovery of dinosaur fossils may be partially responsible for ancient people's beliefs in dragons, there were other factors at play as well. Herpetologist Romulus Whitaker studies snakes, lizards, crocodiles, and other reptiles and amphibians. He says that even today there are living creatures that are known to possess at least one of the characteristics embodied in dragons. For example, he says, the story about St. George features a dragon said to be terrorizing a town and eating people. According to Whitaker, the dragon in that story may have been inspired by a Nile River crocodile, whose long spiky body and whiplike tail can grow to as long as 20 feet (6.1 m), move at speeds up to 10 miles an hour (16.1 kph), and weigh more than 1,000 pounds (453.6 kg).

Moreover, according to Whitaker, Nile crocs, with their eerie eyes and mouths full of sharp teeth, are responsible for more than 100 human deaths each year. Furthermore, according to researchers at the Smithsonian Institution in Washington, DC, Nile crocodiles sometimes lift their bellies off the ground as they walk, an unusual sight that could be misinterpreted. Says science writer Joseph Stromberg, "A giant, lumbering croc? Might be easy to mistake for a dragon."[35]

Dragon lore also includes stories of dragons that sleep for years and dwell in caves. Once awake, they are very, very hungry and equally dangerous to cross paths with. In the natural world, Whitaker points out, there is a peculiar creature known as the

Ancient dragon tales from Africa might be traced to the activities of the Nile crocodile. This long, powerful beast has been known to attack humans, and it can propel itself on land by lifting its body off the ground and lumbering forward on its clawed feet.

What Seventeenth-Century People Believed

In the 1600s a new theory about dragons and how they came to be gained popularity. It was called the Spermatick Principle, and it was an attempt to explain how dragons could simultaneously have the physical attributes of several different animals. According to the theory, all that was needed for new animals to be conceived was the presence of sperm; the egg was considered an afterthought, a source of food for the developing embryo. The Spermatick Principle held that it was possible for sperm from different types of animals (birds, bats, and snakes, for example) to commingle, producing a hybrid creature. According to Donald G. McNeil Jr., a science reporter for the *New York Times*, it was believed that sperm evaporated into the air and when it rained it would settle in the nests of eagles and vultures. With luck, it was believed the offspring produced would be a winged snake.

olm, which has also been referred to as a baby dragon. Found in caves in Slovenia and Croatia in southern Europe, the olm is an 8- to 12-inch (20- to 30-cm), pale, sightless salamander that has been known to live for up to a century and can survive for as long as a decade between meals. This truly bizarre amphibian, known for its excellent sense of hearing and smell, typically eats insects, snails, and crabs—but not people. Yet it is easy to imagine that an unexpected encounter with an olm in a dark cave would definitely inspire thoughts of having seen a monster.

The Flying Lizard and King Cobra

Another lizard that is said to resemble a dragon lives in the rainforests of India. The lizard makes its home high up in the trees. Hardly the size of a dragon, though, the lizard spans a mere nine inches (23 cm) in length. Known familiarly as the Western Ghats flying lizard or the Southern flying lizard, the Latin name for the beast is *Draco dussumieri*. These reptiles are masters of camouflage with a definitive dragon-like appearance. Mostly the lizards dine on ants that live in the trees. When prodded or provoked, they rely on a large skin membrane attached to their rib cage to glide from tree to tree, resembling a tiny dragon in flight. Whitaker speculates that explorers who witnessed the sight of *Draco dussumieri* in flight might have embellished their stories with some flights of their own imaginations.

Besides flying, living in bodies of water, and devouring people, dragons have long been credited with the ability to ensure that no one disturbs the treasure they are guarding. Here Whitaker speculates that king cobras may have been the inspiration for linking dragons and treasure protection. Real-life Asian princes used king cobras, which can reach 18 feet (5.5 m) in length, as security systems. In the imaginations of many people, king cobras—or spitting cobras, which can project their venom into a victim's eyes—may not be that far removed from fire-breathing dragons. After all, their venom is potent enough to kill an elephant or several dozen people over the reptile's lifetime.

> **"There are certainly some accounts that sound very like garbled travelers tales of say, pythons; there are stories of dragons that wound themselves round the thing they were attacking. Certainly once people had the idea of a dragon, a lot of things got mapped on to that idea."[37]**
>
> *—University of York biologist Peter Hogarth.*

Whitaker also points out that king cobras may have sparked people's imaginations because it was not unusual for them to encounter the snakes in the course of their everyday activities. Cobras feed on rats, which feed on garbage, which can often be found in the vicinity of human settlements. "We find [cobras] in people's houses and gardens, in wells and pump houses, seeking shelter,"[36] he says.

Hogarth adds that many types of snakes have likely been confused with dragons over the centuries. He says, "There are certainly some accounts that sound very like garbled travelers tales of say, pythons; there are stories of dragons that wound themselves round the thing they were attacking. Certainly once people had the idea of a dragon, a lot of things got mapped on to that idea."[37]

Yet another living creature that might have inspired belief in dragons is the whale. Stromberg suggests that since whales spend nearly all of their lives underwater, ancient explorers may have been shocked when spotting them coming up for air. Given the mammoth sizes of whales, it is possible ancient mariners may have assumed they were monsters. Moreover, he says, whale bones that were found beached on the shore may have further confirmed people's suspicions that the giant bones were all that was left of a dead land-based dragon.

Komodo Dragons

There are animals that resemble dragons far more closely than the tiny flying lizards of India, the crocodiles of the Nile River, the king cobras of Asian countries, and the huge whales of the ocean. In fact, these animals are actually named dragons.

The Komodo dragon of Indonesia is a large lizard that can grow to over eight feet long. Its bite is strong, and its stinky saliva contains a toxin that prevents blood clotting, leaving wounded prey to bleed to death. The animal's armor-like hide and foul-smelling breath are traits it shares with dragons of myth.

The Komodo dragon, a fierce monitor lizard found only in some islands in Southeast Asia, is the largest of all lizards. It was virtually unknown to scientists until about 1926. That year the American Museum of Natural History sent an expedition to the island of Komodo in Indonesia to study them. Before that time, maps made of the area by ancient explorers carried the words "Here Be Dragons."

Komodo dragons can live for up to fifty years. They can span up to 8.5 feet (2.6 m) in length and weigh as much as 360 pounds (163.3 kg). They have sharp teeth and claws and can run as fast as 12 miles an hour (19.3 kph). Komodos have dark gray, yellow, and orange body scales with dark bands of color that spiral around their tails. They are natural predators to be reckoned with. Claudio Ciofi, a biologist at the University of Florence in Italy, describes the ordeal of attempting to capture a Komodo dragon:

> Slaughter a goat. Cut it up. Enlist a few strong friends to hoist three ten-foot-long [3 m] steel traps, grab bags of goat meat, and trek a few miles up and down knee-punishing hills. Ignore the 90-plus-degree [32°+C] heat that wraps you up and steams you like a dumpling. Set up the first trap with hunks of flesh and hang a few meat bags in trees to "scent" the air. Hike another couple of miles. Lay another trap. Cover three or four more miles [5–6 km], repeat. Return to camp; fill a bucket with cold water and dump it over your head. Sleep. Revisit each trap in the morning and afternoon for the next two days. They'll likely be empty, but if you're lucky, you'll draw near, and there it will be: the world's biggest lizard, a grim-faced giant known as the Komodo dragon.[38]

Fierce Predators

Komodo dragons are known to ambush their prey. They attack the softest flesh, typically the belly, or they may attack the legs of their prey. Their mouths drip with venomous saliva. When the saliva enters the wound of the victim, it prevents the blood from clotting.

Therefore, the bites cause excessive bleeding. Even if the dragon's victim manages to escape, chances are it won't live long. In dense jungles, watering holes are infested with deadly bacteria, meaning the open wounds are likely to become infected. Lurking nearby is the Komodo dragon, waiting patiently for its prey to die.

Not only is the dragon's saliva deadly but it is also foul smelling. The dragon's sense of smell is so keen that it can detect blood or rotting flesh miles away. Although Komodo dragons typically prey on goats, pigs, and deer, attacks on humans are not unknown. Many of those attacks have been fatal.

One victim of a dragon attack is Maen, an Indonesian employed as a ranger in Komodo National Park where the endangered lizards live in a protective environment. As part of his job Maen spends a lot of time in the office. One morning in 2009, while sitting at his desk, he looked down to see that lurking near his sandal-clad foot was a dragon. Apparently the hungry dragon had spent the night in the office looking for food, seizing the opportunity to go inside when another staff member left the office door open. Once he spotted the dragon under his desk, Maen knew he was in trouble. He says, "I think that if I [did] not pull my leg, the dragon will bite and swallow. So I tried to pull my leg but the dragon follow and I look and see a tail moving over there. And I think this is a problem for me. And I pull my leg too fast and it got trapped in the table and then the dragon bite."[39]

Fortunately Maen knew what to do next. He used his free foot to apply pressure on the dragon and his hands to pry open the dragon's mouth enough to remove his foot. By now, coworkers had arrived and were able to pull the dragon away from Maen. To treat the bites to his foot and his hand, Maen faced six hours of emergency care, a week-long hospitalization, and another six months of rehabilitation before he was able to return to his job at the preserve. He is mindful that the lizard that bit him is still out there and not to be underestimated. Maen says, "But I think now he'll be bigger."[40]

"Smoking" Beetles

At least Maen did not have to contend with a beast that breathes actual fire. In nature there is no animal that can do that. However, scientists say that one beetle comes close: the bombardier beetle, which when provoked can emit an impressive 500 explosions per second of a boiling hot, poisonous spray from its hindquarters. Scientists describe this discharge as similar to a machine gun in its rapid fire and precise delivery. But exactly how the unremarkable-looking beetle accomplishes its dragon-like feat was never completely understood until recently when researchers gathered hundreds of the beetles together and X-rayed them as they were provoked into releasing their sprays.

The beetles' bodies contain separate chambers containing two nasty chemicals that when combined lead to an explosion. When the beetles are calm their abdominal muscles prevent the chemicals from merging. In their aroused state a valve releases the two chemicals into another chamber where combustion takes place under pressure that builds until the spray is released in the presence of an enemy. Typical enemies of the beetles, which are found on American soil, are ants, frogs, and spiders. At 212 degrees Fahrenheit (100°C), the spray delivered by the beetles is hot enough to burn the skin and is accompanied by a "pfft" sound similar to what one hears when using an aerosol spray can.

While no one is suggesting that encounters with bombardier beetles ever inspired dragon tales, there has been some interesting speculation on what other natural phenomena may have led to such stories that were popular in medieval times. Science writer Matt Kaplan suggests that ancient people may have sought a reasonable explanation for the sudden conflagration that occured when a wildfire met a dry field of grass or produced an intense explosion when it came into contact with pockets of natural gas. In a similar vein, people digging in the earth for coal while carrying torches might also have inadvertently created an explosion that they attributed to the presence of an unseen dragon; however, the true culprit was methane or hydrogen sulfide gas, he says. Both gases are capable of killing people who breathe them and the latter also gives off a nasty odor.

In fact, Kaplan says a methane explosion may explain the eruption of fire blasting forth from the dragon's lair in *Beowulf* when Beowulf and Wiglaf approach the monster's lair for the ultimate battle. Centuries ago, Kaplan says, it was not unusual

> "The dragon in *Beowulf* is nothing more than a burst of methane escaping from a tomb that a torch-holding grave robber opened up and accidentally set ablaze. . . . There *was* no creature, just one imagined by those who could not comprehend flames leaping out of a burial mound all on their own."[41]
>
> — *Science journalist Matt Kaplan.*

for people to use caves as burial chambers for their deceased loved ones. In addition to the deceased's possessions (perhaps the treasure guarded by the dragon), people also deposited the carcasses of pets and horses to accompany loved ones into the afterlife. Methane-producing bacteria formed and expanded in the carcasses. If some hapless grave robber happened to enter the cave with a torch, the methane could ignite resulting in a fiery explosion. Kaplan says, "The dragon in *Beowulf* is nothing more than a burst of methane escaping from a tomb that a torch-holding grave robber opened up and accidentally set ablaze. . . . There *was* no creature, just one imagined by those who could not comprehend flames leaping out of a burial mound all on their own."[41]

Geology and Climate Explanations

These methane explosions may provide a good reason for why much of the mythology surrounding dragons developed first in medieval Europe rather than the Middle East. The dry and sandy soil found in the Middle East does not trap gases the same way that the moister soils of Europe do. So there is a smaller chance that a gassy buildup of methane would explode.

In addition, the natural event known as the Aurora Borealis may have prompted imaginations to run wild, conjuring up fears of dragons. The Aurora is a dramatic swirling light show of green, red, yellow, and blue caused by solar winds striking atoms in the earth's atmosphere. In 1621, French astronomer Pierre Gassendi identified the Aurora as a natural light show. Before then, though, people may have imagined dragons as the cause. Says Hogarth, "Actually, if you think of dragons flying in the air and then you see the Aurora Borealis or even a lightning storm, it's not too much of a stretch to link the two things together: they're not just dragons in the air, they're fiery dragons. How else would you explain the aurora or lightning if you didn't understand it?"[42]

In the end, the scientific search for answers for why people have long believed in dragons is just as interesting as their belief in dragons themselves. Like the young boy in the Children's Museum of Indianapolis, it seems entirely plausible that anybody could be seduced into believing the dragon myth had they been confronted with unknown scary fossils; encounters with unfamiliar living animals such as crocodiles, monitor lizards, whales, and olms; or folktales shared from generation to generation. These factors kept dragon legends alive as they simultaneously provided the best explanations available at the time for mysteries for which science would eventually provide answers.

Chapter 4

Why Are People So Fascinated by Dragons?

"I believe in everything until it's disproved. So I believe in fairies, the myths, dragons. It all exists, even if it's in your mind. Who's to say that dreams and nightmares aren't as real as the here and now?"

—John Lennon, legendary songwriter and member of the Beatles.

Quoted in Inspire 99, "Inspirational Quotes: John Lennon—I Believe In Everything, Fairies, Myths and Dragons," March 3, 2015. http://inspire99.com.

"These things we're going to see don't, like, actually exist, right?"

—Lacy, a young girl about to tour the American Museum of Natural History exhibit "Mythic Creatures: Dragons, Unicorns, and Mermaids."

Quoted in Adam Gopnik, "Creature Feature," *New Yorker*, June 4, 2007, p. 38.

Despite their ancient origins dragons remain firmly entrenched in twenty-first-century life. For example, in major American cities with significant Asian American populations, revelers carrying huge paper and fabric dragons can be seen during holiday celebrations snaking their way through streets accompanied by smoke and explosions and the smell of gunpowder. Meanwhile on the screens of multiplexes across the country, beastly dragons continue to guard treasures in caves while alternatively bragging about their prowess and spitting fire.

One of the most familiar dragons in popular culture is Smaug, a most vile creature who sprang from the imagination of J.R.R. Tolkien, a British college professor who wrote the medieval fantasy novel *The Hobbit* in 1937. This classic story features in a central role the greedy and possessive Smaug, who talks, flies, and breathes fire. The book has been adapted into a three-film presentation, the most recent installment being *The Hobbit: The Battle of the Five Armies*, which was released in 2014.

> **"It is rather disappointing that, when the natural world was thoroughly explored in the nineteenth century, no true awe-inspiring dragons were brought to light. . . . How much better it would have been if only some of them had turned out to be real living and breathing creatures."[43]**
>
> *—British zoologist Desmond Morris.*

The dragons concocted by twenty-first-century author Donita K. Paul are far friendlier than Smaug. Paul is the author of the Dragon-Keeper Chronicles series of books. Paul's stories follow the adventures of a former slave girl named Kale, who is charged with guarding the eggs of dragons. When the baby dragons hatch, they are quite friendly and humorous—far from the type of evil monster envisioned by Tolkien. Paul's dragons are so likable that she created a special day devoted to dragons—Appreciate a Dragon Day, which takes place every January 16.

What is perhaps most remarkable about the dragons like Smaug or those created by Paul is that well into the twenty-first century, the creatures continue to dominate popular culture, despite the fact that most people stopped believing in dragons hundreds of years ago. Says noted British zoologist Desmond Morris,

> It is rather disappointing that, when the natural world was thoroughly explored in the nineteenth century, no true awe-inspiring dragons were brought to light. . . . How much better it would have been if only some of them had turned out to be real living and breathing creatures that we could, at great risk and with enormous difficulty, encounter and marvel at today.[43]

Creationists: Dragons Were Real

Despite the assertion by Morris and other zoologists that dragons simply do not exist nor have ever existed, there are some true believers—those who contend that flesh-and-blood men and women really did confront actual dragons as depicted in the Bible. Holding that view is Darek Isaacs, an author and filmmaker who believes the Bible is the literal word of God. Isaacs and others, known as creationists, accept the stories of the Bible as fact. The term *creationist* stems from the view that, according to the Book of Genesis, man, woman, and all the creatures of the earth were created by God in six days. According to a 2012 poll by the Gallup Organization, a highly respected polling organization based in Princeton, New Jersey, some 46 percent of Americans regard themselves as creationists.

Creationists believe God created humankind in its present form sometime within the past 10,000 years. The views of creationists contrast with those of scientists who maintain that the universe and all life forms evolved over a period of about 4.5 billion years.

> **"The Bible speaks about dragons. Our authority—everything we do, we have to measure by the word of God. That is what I believe. So we have to go to the Bible, and the Bible speaks about dragons."[44]**
>
> *—Creationist Darek Isaacs.*

But for Isaacs and his fellow believers in the literal interpretation of the Bible, everything that is detailed in the Bible actually happened, and that includes the stories it tells that relate to dragons. Isaacs says, "The Bible speaks about dragons. Our authority—everything we do, we have to measure by the word of God. That is what I believe. So we have to go to the Bible, and the Bible speaks about dragons."[44] For example, Isaacs and other creationists have no doubt whatsoever that the biblical figure Job really did confront a scaly, toothsome dragon that sprang from the sea. The Book of Job 41:19 describes the monster: "Out of his mouth go burning lamps, and sparks of fire leap out. Out of his nostrils goeth smoke, as out of a seething pot or caldron. His breath kindleth coals, and a flame goeth out of his mouth."

According to Christians who interpret the word of the Bible as literal truth, dragons did exist because scripture refers to them. The Book of Revelation, for example, describes Michael and other angels battling a dragon (identified with Satan) during the war in heaven.

Isaacs blames skeptics and modern biblical scholars for demoting dragons to mythological status. "Modern translators simply could not allow the dragon to have an authentic seat at the biblical tables in these modern sophisticated times," Isaacs insists. "Therefore, in poor form, a blind eye is turned to that scaly and unwanted dinner guest. . . . I will shine a spotlight for all to see the Bible speaks of dragons as real."[45]

Views at Odds with Science

As the Gallup Poll illustrates, creationism is accepted by many Americans. In fact creationism is an integral part of the curricula taught at many Christian-based schools in America. And many students who attend those schools use textbooks in which encounters with dragons are presented as fact. An excerpt from *Life Science Student Text*, published by Bob Jones University Press in 2007, reads,

> [Is] it possible that a fire-breathing animal really existed? Today some scientists are saying yes. They have found large chambers in certain dinosaur skulls. The large skull chambers could have contained special chemical-producing glands. When the animal forced the chemicals out of its mouth or nose, these substances may have combined and produced fire and smoke.[46]

Those who do not adhere to creationist views point out that before a scientific theory is accepted as fact it must undergo close study, sometimes for years. Typically, numerous scientists test the theory using a variety of methods, looking for legitimate evidence that supports the theory. Chemical and biological analyses are employed, and these analyses are often repeated several times to make sure the same conclusions are reached by different researchers. None of that, they assert, has been applied to the creationist view, including the assertion that dragons once roamed the planet. Jon P. Alston, a professor of sociology at Texas A&M University, suggests that the creationist belief in dragons merits as little legitimacy as the creationist belief that humans and dinosaurs once shared the planet. (Paleontologists insist that dinosaurs were extinct some 62 million years before the first humans evolved.) Says Alston, "The issue whether humans and dinosaurs lived at the same time illustrates both the scientific creationists' resistance to facts and how their theorizing falls outside established science. . . . Scientific creationists believe legends of dragons and other monsters reflect a time when dinosaurs and humans shared the world."[47]

Inherited Fears

Regardless of whether stories of dragons are drawn from the Bible or from myths, until authors like Paul made dragons into harmless creatures, for the most part dragons had been portrayed over time as scary and frightful beasts. Modern scientists wonder whether the frightening qualities of dragons may be resonating in people's subconscious minds, triggering beliefs in the creatures as real.

The late Carl Sagan, noted astronomer and certainly no believer in dragons, nevertheless accepted the theory that some fears are hardwired into people's brains. In his book, *The Dragons of Eden: Speculations on the Evolution of Human Intelligence*, Sagan points out that parents often make a "shhhh" sound to quiet their noisy children. He wondered whether that sound has remained hidden in people's subconscious minds because their ancestors learned to be frightened of a similar sound made by snakes and lizards. "Is it only an accident that the common human sounds commanding silence or attracting attention seem strangely imitative of the hissing of reptiles?"[48] Sagan asks. He adds, then, that it was certainly possible for the dragon believers of hundreds of years ago to pass on a subconscious fear of dragons to their modern-day descendants.

Sagan was not the first scientist to speculate on the existence of inherited fears. More than 150 years ago, Charles Darwin expressed a similar opinion. The British naturalist, whose 1859 book *On the Origin of Species*, established the science of evolution, suggested, "May we not suspect that the vague but very real fears of children, which are quite independent of experience, are inherited effects of real dangers and abject superstitions during ancient savage times?"[49] In other words, Darwin believed, a fear of dragons could be handed down from generation to generation—even though there never really were dragons to begin with.

From Monkeys to Dragons

Paul A. Trout, professor emeritus at Montana State University, suggests that another fear that may be hardwired into people's brains is the absolute terror of being eaten—by anything. And certainly many stories about dragons have featured frightening scenes of hapless victims gobbled up by fearsome dragons.

> Every day over the course of several million years our ancestors saw (and heard) living creatures being torn apart and devoured by hungry animals—with some victims still kicking as they were eviscerated and dismembered. No wonder our brains are wired to make us dread this awful fate, and that the stories we tell ourselves reflect this dread and attempt to express it . . . The archetype of the [dragon] is an expression of this primal fear writ large, exaggerated and intensified to an outlandish degree."[50]

University of Central Florida anthropologist David E. Jones has examined this fear and concluded that three animals—the eagle, leopard, and snake—represented very real threats to people in past societies. He suggests those people may have subconsciously combined the three animals into the image of a dragon. Jones says he developed the theory as he planned a lecture on the behavior of a small monkey known as the vervet. Research into the habits of the vervet found the animal makes separate warning calls to alert other monkeys that specific predators are approaching. He says,

> After completing my notes for the vervet lecture, I was absent-mindedly gathering the books I had used when one fell open to a page headed "The Vervets' Predators." Images of an eagle, a leopard, and a snake were featured. Suddenly, in my mind's eye, the three predator images merged. The leopard body took on the outer look of the python, resulting in a large reptilian body with four clawed feet and a mouth full of sharp teeth. When the wings of the martial eagle attached to the shoulders of the blended leopard/python I saw a dragon![51]

Jones suggests that the vervets' survival as a species was predicated on their ability to shield themselves from predators,

Dragon Bones as Medicine

Americans who find themselves suffering from diarrhea or an upset stomach may find relief after purchasing a product such as Pepto-Bismol, which is made from the digestive enzyme pepsin and zinc salts, among other ingredients. However, when Chinese people suffer from similar complaints, they might go to one of their pharmacies for dragon bone powders.

Known also as *longgu*, the fossilized bones and teeth are actually from dinosaurs, not dragons. Still, dragon bone powders are administered in China as treatments for dysentery, coughs, depression, headaches, and dizziness. Most of the powdered dragon bones and teeth come from the town of Shanxi, where many fossils can be found. Lei Xiao, a medical scholar who lived in the fifth century, wrote down his formula for turning dragon bones into medicines:

> For using dragon's bones, first cook odorous plants; bathe the bones in hot water, pound them to a powder and put this in bags of gauze. Take a couple of young swallows and, after taking out their intestines and stomach, put the bags in the swallows and hang them over a well. After one night take the bags out of the swallows, rub the powder and mix it into medicines for strengthening the kidneys. The efficacy of such a medicine is as it were divine.

Quoted in Ernest Ingersoll, *Dragons and Dragon Lore: A Worldwide Study of Dragons in History, Art and Legend*. Seattle, WA: CreateSpace, 2012, p. 46.

and over time the vervet brain became hardwired to instinctively do that job. In a similar fashion, he asserts, humans may have evolved a dragon instinct to protect themselves from the few animals that are big and strong enough to eat them. He says, "The word dragon was formed by the nature of our own shadowy progenitors' encounters with the creatures who hunted them over millions of years."[52]

But Paul Jordan-Smith, an expert on folklore, takes issue with a number of Jones's assertions, finding that for most people, an eagle, leopard, and snake simply do not add up to a dragon. Jordan-Smith also doubts whether the fear of a specific mythological creature—a dragon—can be hardwired into people's brains and handed down from generation to generation, perhaps for thousands of years. Says Jordan-Smith, "David Jones . . . should have known better than to tangle with dragons, bereft as he seems to be of a much-needed arsenal of data, clarity, and logic."[53]

Fear of Snakes

Despite Jordan-Smith's criticism, one of the animals Jones says is responsible for making people believe in dragons is the snake.

Humanity's fear of snakes might be grounded in prehistoric times when early humans slept in shelters that were easily accessible to small creatures. Because dragons have some resemblance to serpents, it is possible that people's fear of these creatures is related.

Fear of snakes is, in fact, a scientifically accepted phobia. Psychologists have even given fear of snakes a name: ophidiophobia.

Science journalist Matt Kaplan suggests that fear of snakes could be another fear that has been hard-wired into people's brains for thousands of years. Today most people live in cities and are likely never to see a snake in their lives unless perhaps they visit a zoo. And yet many city dwellers find themselves suffering from ophidiophobia. Perhaps, Kaplan suggests, their distant ancestors many generations ago lived in jungles or forests and slept in huts—the type of dwelling a snake could enter at any time, unseen. He says, "We don't think of them as dangerous today, because we don't sleep in beds of reeds with doors that don't close."[54]

> **"The word dragon was formed by the nature of our own shadowy progenitors' encounters with the creatures who hunted them over millions of years."[52]**
>
> *—University of Central Florida anthropologist David E. Jones.*

Certainly snakes have long been regarded as an inspiration for dragon stories. It is possible that people's ancestors, fretting over whether snakes may enter their huts at night, grew to fear them as much as they feared dragons. Now, generations later, that fear has manifested itself in their descendants as ophidiophobia and also perhaps a fear—and belief—in dragons.

Enjoying a Good Fright

Although people with ophidiophobia prefer not to be around snakes because of the anxiety and stress they would experience due to their phobia, there is no question that a lot of people really do enjoy a good fright. Dean Burnett, a doctor of neuroscience, suggests that dragons continue to fascinate people precisely because they are dangerous. According to Burnett, many people like to be scared, albeit from a safe distance.

There is no clearer evidence of this type of behavior than the box office receipts collected by Hollywood producers, who each year are more than delighted to release horror movies guaranteed to make the audience members shriek. The book sales credited to Stephen King provide more evidence. King is the author of more than fifty novels since the 1970s—many written to shock his readers. By 2015 King's books had sold more than 300 million copies. Burnett says,

> People like danger and risk, and dragons represent this in spades. Also, they're usually very aesthetically pleasing, all majestic and awe-inspiring. But it could also be like how children love dinosaurs; they provide the potential for danger and excitement, but are totally safe because they don't exist . . . The potential for dangerous thrills without ever actually delivering can be very appealing for people."[55]

Friendly Dragons

Author Christopher Paolini made it a point, however, not to scare people with the dragon he created. Paolini is the author of the bestselling novel *Eragon*, which was published in 2002. Paolini began writing the story in 1997 when he was fourteen years old, finishing the book a year later. Three sequels to *Eragon* have followed as well as a movie adaptation that was released in 2005. Paolini had been hooked on medieval stories for years and came up with *Eragon*, a play on the word dragon, as a way to flesh out the fantasy world in which he wished he could live. The book's hero, Eragon, is modeled after Paolini. In the novel Eragon finds and cares for a dragon's egg until it hatches. But in Paolini's dragon story the creature is not an enemy—she is a loving friend named Saphira. In explaining his motivation for making Saphira into a good-hearted dragon, he says,

> I decided to go in a more human direction with Saphira, my dragon, because the more I thought about it, the more I realized that she is raised away from her species, away from her race, in close mental contact with a human. I considered making the dragon more dragon-like, if you will, in its own society, but I haven't had a chance to explore that. I went with a more human element with Saphira while still trying to get a bit of the magic, the alien, of her race.[56]

Game of Thrones' Dragons and Anatomy

The popular TV drama *Game of Thrones* is based on a series of fantasy novels written by George R.R. Martin. Set in the fictional continent of Westeros, *Game of Thrones* features the dragons Drogon, Rhaegal, Viserion, and Balerion. The ultrarealistic dragons and their movements were created using computer-generated imaging techniques as well as some hands-on exploration of a chicken bought at a supermarket.

The dragons are created by the visual effects company Pixomondo. In explaining how the company's artists create the dragons, Pixomondo visual effects supervisor Sven Martin says he first stopped at the supermarket to buy a chicken because he suspected the bone structure of a dragon would be similar to that of the bird. "I was looking for an animal so we can really discover how the muscles underneath should work. I called over all the animators and they all had to just play with the chicken. . . . You could feel how the muscles underneath are moving and what are the restrictions, where the bone can't go. We built our dragons basically the same way." According to Martin, it takes as many as thirty computer animators to create the dragons for each episode.

Quoted in Thomas Johnson, "How *Game of Thrones* Creates Its Dragons," *Washington Post*, March 19, 2015. www.washingtonpost.com.

Paolini's Saphira is portrayed as heroic. So too are the dragons in the animated children's movie *How to Train Your Dragon* and its sequel, both of which are based on popular children's books by author Cressida Cowell. These newer dragons are representative of the way dragons have been evolving in popular culture from their ancient roles as predators. Now, popular culture is portraying them more in the role of companions—with, of course, the exception of Smaug and a few others.

Drogon is the largest and most aggressive of the dragons raised by Daenerys Targaryan in George R.R. Martin's fantasy book series A Song of Ice and Fire. The HBO series Game of Thrones *(based on the books) depicts Drogon by adhering to the traditional motifs of dragons in popular culture.*

In 2014, when *People* magazine compiled a list of the top twenty-four dragons in pop culture, the publication's choices included quite a few that were not scary. These included Dragon, who falls in love with Donkey in the movie *Shrek*; Mushu, the skinny and comical dragon from the animated film *Mulan*; and Falkor, the lucky and furry creature from the film *The Neverending Story*. However, there were some more traditional dragons also making the list, among them Smaug; Drogon, the fearsome beast from the *Game of Thrones* books and TV series; and the extremely vicious Hungarian Horntail from the book and film *Harry Potter and the Goblet of Fire*.

Prism on the Natural World

Despite the ongoing popularity of Smaug and the other evil beasts, reptile expert Romulus Whitaker is pleased with the new, friendlier reputation dragons seem to be developing. He sees a silver lining that others are likely to miss—if people are more comfortable around mythical dragons, they may be more friendly toward real live reptiles.

> Years ago it was pretty hard to get people to empathize even a little bit with scaly, cold-blooded critters; now, thanks a lot to good PR from television, it is easier to get the message of reptile conversation and tolerance across. We have a lot to be thankful to reptiles for, not the least of which is their control of rodents. But besides their utility on the planet, our remaining dragons are needed to excite our senses, to fill every generation with renewed wonder, and to keep us alert for that predator lurking just around the corner!"[57]

Writer James Balm argues that dragons continue to play an important role in helping people come to grips with their own places in the natural world. In his view dragons represent not only people's fear of snakes but also people's desires to domesticate wild animals as past generations have successfully done with wild dogs, wolves, and cats. He says, "To me, dragons reflect an aspect of human psychology and evolution. They are a focus for our fears, and our consequent desires to conquer those fears. They explore our relationship with nature: our fears, our desires, and our insecurities. But as we learn from both fact and fiction, not everything can be tamed."[58]

In the end, what fascinates people most about dragons may be highly individualized, the conclusion reached by fantasy writer Trevor Green. He says,

> So why would anyone read about elves and dwarves, magic and dragons? Each fan might have a different answer, each passionate and thoughtful. For some it might be the magic, a wondrous and ethereal power that can do amazing things, or a dreaded black hole of fear and control, depending on its use. For others it may be the long standing theme of good versus evil, where anyone, no matter how insignificant or poor, may stand up to evil and all its powers, if only given the chance."[59]

"We have a lot to be thankful to reptiles for, not the least of which is their control of rodents. But besides their utility on the planet, our remaining dragons are needed to excite our senses, to fill every generation with renewed wonder, and to keep us alert for that predator lurking just around the corner!"[57]

— Reptile expert Romulus Whitaker.

Dragons have been envisioned by people for thousands of years. Creationists believe they were real and that Bible stories recounting human encounters with dragons are true. Scientists scoff at such beliefs, but many are willing to accept the notion that while dragons may not be real, fear of dragons is very real and has, in fact, been hardwired into people's brains. Regardless of who is right, the dragon—noble or comic, fire breathing or serenely intelligent, lucky presence or harbinger of death—is not likely to disappear from the human world any time soon.

Source Notes

Introduction: Dragons: Myths or Misunderstandings?

1. Quoted in Scott T. Sterling, "Imagine Dragons: Inside the Secret Origins of the Band's Name," *CBS Local*, January 7, 2013. http://kroq.cbslocal.com.
2. David Passes, *Dragon Legends*. London: Pavilion Children's Books, 1993, p. 8.
3. Marco Polo, *The Travels of Marco Polo*. Edinburgh: Oliver & Boyd, 1845, pp. 160–61.
4. Mike Edwards, "Wonders and Whoppers: Following in Marco Polo's Footsteps Through Asia Leads Our Intrepid Author to Some Surprising Conclusions," *Smithsonian*, July 2008. www.smithsonianmag.com.

Chapter One: What Are Dragons?

5. *Aberdeen Bestiary*, "Of the Dragon," Aberdeen University Library, 1995. www.abdn.ac.uk.
6. *Aberdeen Bestiary*, "What Is a Bestiary?" www.abdn.ac.uk.
7. Margaret Weis, "An Image for Nightmares—and Dreams," foreword to, *Dragons: The Myths, Legends, and Lore*, by Doug Niles. Avon, MA: Adams Media, 2013, pp. 6–7.
8. Doug Niles, *Dragons: The Myths, Legends, and Lore*. Avon, MA: Adams Media, 2013, p. 30.

9. Joseph Fontenrose, *Python: A Study of Delphic Myth and Its Origins*. Berkeley: University of California Press, 1980, p. 187.
10. Jonathan Couch, trans., *Pliny's Natural History*. London: Barclay, 1848, p. 17.
11. Couch, *Pliny's Natural History*, p. 18.
12. Arthur Charles Fox-Davies, *A Complete Guide to Heraldry*. New York: Skyhorse, 2007, p. 224.
13. Niles, *Dragons: The Myths, Legends, and Lore*, p. 63.
14. Niles, *Dragons: The Myths, Legends, and Lore*, p. 75.
15. Benjamin Radford, "Are Dragons Real? Facts About Dragons," LiveScience.com, December 10, 2014. www.livescience.com.
16. Quoted in Hype Malaysia, "NagaPutihHoax: White Dragon 'Found' in Malaysia, Apparently," June 24, 2014. http://hype.my.
17. Alessandro Sorrentino, "Dragon Not Real," *The World of Chinese*, June 27, 2014. www.theworldofchinese.com.
18. Andrew J. Hamilton, Robert M. May, and Edward K. Waters, "Here Be Dragons," *Nature*, April 2, 2015, p. 43.

Chapter Two: Encounters with Dragons

19. Robert Graves, *The Greek Myths, Volume II*. Wakefield, RI: Moyer Bell, 1994, p. 108.
20. Karl Shuker, *Dragons: A Natural History*. New York: Barnes & Noble, 2003, pp. 106–8.
21. Quoted in Niles, *Dragons: The Myths, Legends, and Lore,* p. 40.
22. Quoted in William Witherle Lawrence, "The Dragon and His Lair in *Beowulf*," *PMLA*, vol. 33, no. 4, 1918, p. 550. www.jstor.org/stable/456981?seq=4#page_scan_tab_contents.
23. Quoted in Henry Spackman Pancoast, *English Prose and Verse from Beowulf to Stevenson*. New York: Holt, 1915, p. 7.

24. Thomas Meyer, *Beowulf: A Translation*. New York: Punctum, 2012, p. 248.
25. Lewis Warsh and Michael Spring, *Beowulf*. Woodbury, NY: Barron's, 1984, p. 16.
26. Christine Rauer, *Beowulf and the Dragon: Parallels and Analogues*. Suffolk, UK: Boydell & Brewer, 2000, p. 24.
27. Fontenrose, *Python: A Study of Delphic Myth and Its Origins*, p. 516.
28. Fontenrose, *Python: A Study of Delphic Myth and Its Origins*, p. 517.
29. Quoted in Niles, *Dragons: The Myths, Legends, and Lore*, p. 83.

Chapter Three: The Science of Dragons

30. Patrick Saulsbury, "Discovering a New Dinosaur Species: *Dracorex Hogwartsia*," August 1, 2006. http://veterinarymedicine.dvm360.com.
31. Saulsbury, "Discovering a New Dinosaur Species."
32. Humanities at Stanford, "Dinosaurs and Dragons, Oh My. Stanford Fossil Historian Links Dinosaur Bones to Mythological Creatures," October 2, 2008. http://shc.stanford.edu.
33. Humanities at Stanford, "Dinosaurs and Dragons, Oh My. Stanford Fossil Historian Links Dinosaur Bones to Mythological Creatures."
34. Quoted in Donald G. McNeil Jr., "From Many Imaginations, One Fearsome Creature," *New York Times*, April 29, 2003. www.nytimes.com.
35. Joseph Stromberg, "Where Did Dragons Come From?," *Smithsonian*, January 23, 2012. www.smithsonianmag.com.
36. Quoted in Jamie James, *The Snake Charmer: A Life and Death in Pursuit of Knowledge*. New York: Hyperion, 2008, Kindle edition.

37. Owen Williams, "Could Dragons Exist? We Ask an Expert," *Empire*, December 20, 2013. www.empireonline.com.

38. Jennifer S. Holland, "Once Upon a Dragon: Earth's Most Monstrous Lizard Faces an Uncertain Future," *National Geographic*, January 2014. http://ngm.nationalgeographic.com.

39. Quoted in Michael Turtle, "I Was Attacked by a Dragon and Survived," October 20, 2012. www.timetravelturtle.com.

40. Quoted in Turtle, "I Was Attacked by a Dragon and Survived."

41. Matt Kaplan, *Medusa's Gaze and Vampire's Bite*. New York: Scribner, 2012, p. 113.

42. Quoted in Williams, "Could Dragons Exist? We Ask an Expert."

Chapter Four: Why Are People So Fascinated by Dragons?

43. Quoted in Shuker, *Dragons: A Natural History*, p. 8.

44. Quoted in Meredith Bennett-Smith, "Creationist Darek Isaacs Calls Dragons Real, Says They Lived in Biblical Times," *Huffington Post*, August 15, 2013. www.huffingtonpost.com.

45. Quoted in Bennett-Smith, "Creationist Darek Isaacs Calls Dragons Real, Says They Lived in Biblical Times."

46. Deanna Pan, "14 Wacky 'Facts' Kids Will Learn in Louisiana's Voucher Schools," *Mother Jones*, August 7, 2012. www.motherjones.com.

47. Jon P. Alston, *The Scientific Case Against Scientific Creationism*. Lincoln, NE: iUniverse, 2003, p. 78.

48. Carl Sagan, *The Dragons of Eden: Speculations on the Evolution of Human Intelligence*. New York: Random House, 2012, p. 150.

49. Charles Darwin, *Charles Darwin: An Anthology*. New Brunswick, NJ: Transaction, p. 406.

50. Paul A. Trout, "How We Invented Monsters," *Salon*, December 3, 2011. www.salon.com.

51. David E. Jones, *An Instinct for Dragons*. New York: Routledge, 2000, p. 4.

52. Quoted in Alan Boyle, "Why We Love to Fear Dragons," *NBC News*, March 30, 2012. http://cosmiclog.nbcnews.com.

53. Paul Jordan-Smith, "An Instinct for Dragons," *Western Folklore*, Spring 2002, p. 123.

54. Quoted in Keith Wagstaff, "Could the 'Game of Thrones' Dragons Fly and Breathe Fire?," *NBC News*, April 9, 2015. www.nbcnews.com.

55. Dean Burnett, "Here Be Dragons: The Science of the Flying Reptiles," *Guardian* (Manchester), April 24, 2014. www.theguardian.com.

56. Quoted in Dave Weich, "Philip Pullman, Tamora Pierce, and Christopher Paolini Talk Fantasy Fiction," Inheritance Cycle, July 31, 2003. www.alagaesia.com.

57. Quoted in *PBS,* "The Dragon Chronicles: Interview: Rom Whitaker, Reptile Expert," September 18, 2011. www.pbs.org.

58. James Balm, "The Psychology of Myth, Popularity, and Obsession," BioMed Central, May 5, 2014. http://blogs.biomedcentral.com.

59. Trevor Green, "Why Fantasy Is Important," *Beyond Dragons and Wizards*, September 2011. http://beyonddragonsandwizards.blogspot.com.

For Further Research

Books

Ruth Bjorklund, *Komodo Dragons*. New York: Scholastic, 2012.

Joyce Hargreaves, *A Little History of Dragons*. New York: Walker, 2009.

Darek Isaacs, *Dragons or Dinosaurs: Creation or Evolution?* Alachua, FL: Bridge-Logos, 2010.

Matt Kaplan, *Medusa's Gaze and Vampire's Bite: The Science of Monsters*. New York: Scribner, 2012.

Adrienne Mayor, *The First Fossil Hunters: Dinosaurs, Mammoths and Myth in Greek and Roman Times*. Princeton, NJ: Princeton University Press, 2011.

Carla Mooney, *Dragons*. San Diego, CA: ReferencePoint, 2011.

Doug Niles, *Dragons: The Myths, Legends, and Lore*. Avon, MA: Adams Media, 2013.

Periodicals

Judith Duffy, "Dragons and Monsters, Gods and Heroes: Did Dinosaur Fossils Inspire Ancient Legends?," *Read*, March 2012.

Anita Gates, "They Didn't Exist. But Could They Have?," *New York Times*, March 19, 2005.

Jennifer S. Holland, "Once Upon a Dragon: Earth's Most Monstrous Lizard Faces an Uncertain Future," *National Geographic*, January 2014.

Donald G. McNeil Jr., "From Many Imaginations, One Fearsome Creature," *New York Times*, April 29, 2003.

Joseph Stromberg, "Where Did Dragons Come From?," *Smithsonian*, January 23, 2012.

Gemma Tarlach, "The Science Behind Mythological Dragons," *Discover*, December 11, 2013.

Ed Yong, "The Olm: The Blind Cave Salamander That Lives to 100," *Discover*, July 20, 2010.

Videos

The Dragon Chronicles (www.pbs.org/wnet/nature/the-dragon-chronicles-video-full-episode/4563). PBS's January 10, 2009, fifty-minute special follows reptile expert Romulus Whitaker as he roams the world to identify living creatures that likely inspired people's belief in dragons. Among them are the olm, the Komodo dragon, and the miniature flying lizard *Draco dussumieri*.

"Dragons: A Fantasy Made Real" (www.animalplanet.com/tv-shows/other/videos/dragons-were-dragons-real). Short clip about the making of the 2005 Animal Planet special *Dragons: A Fantasy Made Real*. The video features interviews with the producers and other professionals associated with the program as well as glimpses of the CGI dragons depicted.

How A Dragon Kills (www.youtube.com/watch?v=bSkJfA3XxOA). Smithsonian Channel's under-four-minute video details the stalking and eating habits of Komodo dragons. The graphic footage follows the exploits of venom expert Dr. Bryan Fry, head of the University of Queensland's Venom Evolution Laboratory in Queensland, Australia.

Websites

American Museum of Natural History (www.amnh.org/exhibitions/past-exhibitions/mythic-creatures/dragons-creatures-of-power). Website contains information from a past exhibit entitled "Dragons: Creatures of Power." Visitors can find information about European, Asian, and imperial dragons, their nature and history, and discover fun facts about dragons.

Beowulf in Hypertext (www.humanities.mcmaster.ca/~beowulf). Website dedicated to the epic poem *Beowulf*, put together under the supervision of an English professor from McMaster University in Hamilton, Ontario, Canada. Visitors can read the entire text of the poem and find information about its characters, authorship, and history. There are links to other websites about *Beowulf*.

Komodo National Park (www.komodonationalpark.org). Established in 1980 to conserve the endangered Komodo dragons and their environment, Komodo National Park maintains a website that tells visitors about the park, its villages, and inhabitants. View a map of the park, and learn how people can arrange a visit and what they might see when they do so.

Theoi Greek Mythology (www.theoi.com). Website explores mythology in classic literature and art with many details on the four types of dragons in Greek mythology. Learn about the Hydra, the dragon of the Golden Fleece, the python, the Ethiopian sea-monster, and the she-dragon Echidna.

Index

Picture Credits

Cover: Thinkstock Images

Associated Press: 39

© Stefano Blanchetti/Corbis: 25

Depositphotos: 46

© Gonzales Photo/Marcus Andreassen/The Hell Gate/ Corbis: 5

HBO/Photofest: 64

Redibis/Shutterstock.com: 33

Ruskpp/Shutterstock.com: 55

Thinkstock Images: 10, 19, 43, 60

Historiated initial 'L' depicting Pliny the Elder, detail of frontispiece to Book I, from the 'Historia Naturalis' (vellum) (detail of 84902), Italian School, (15th century)/Biblioteca Marciana, Venice, Italy/Bridgeman Images: 15

Scene from Beowulf (gouache on paper), Howat, Andrew (20th Century)/Private Collection /© Look and Learn/ Bridgeman Images: 28

About the Author

Gail Snyder is a freelance writer and advertising copywriter who has written nearly twenty books for young readers. She lives in Chalfont, Pennsylvania, with her husband, Hal Marcovitz.